hover car racer
CRASH COURSE

MATTHEW REILLY

Illustrated by Pablo Raimondi

Simon & Schuster Books for Young Readers
New York   London   Toronto   Sydney

For Matt Martin

SIMON & SCHUSTER BOOKS FOR YOUNG READERS
An imprint of Simon & Schuster Children's Publishing Division
1230 Avenue of the Americas, New York, New York 10020

Text previously published in Australia in 2004 by Pan Macmillan Australia Pty Limited
SIMON & SCHUSTER BOOKS FOR YOUNG READERS is a trademark
of Simon & Schuster, Inc.
Book design by Daniel Roode
The text for this book is set in Sabon.
Manufactured in the United States of America
2 4 6 8 10 9 7 5 3 1
CIP data for this book is available from the Library of Congress.
ISBN 1-4169-0225-2

Also by Matthew Reilly

Ice Station
Temple
Contest
Area 7
Scarecrow

Imagine twenty fighter jets racing around a twisting, turning aerial track, ducking and weaving and overtaking at insanely high speeds, and you've just imagined a hover car race.

—Rand Thomasson
three-time hover car racing champion

PART I

JASON AND THE ARGONAUT

A FEW YEARS FROM NOW . . .

INDO-PACIFIC REGIONAL CHAMPIONSHIPS: GULF OF CARPENTARIA AUSTRALIA (GATE RACE)

 Gates

Gulf of Carpentaria

• Halls
Creek

Sydney

AUSTRALIA

100 Point Zone

90 Point Zone

GRANDSTANDS

SANDBARS

60 Point Zone

50 Point Zone

80 Point Zone

40 Point Zone

30 Point Zone

SWAMP

70 Point Zone

20 Point Zone

10 Point Zone

START/FINISH and PIT AREA

INDO-PACIFIC REGIONAL CHAMPIONSHIPS
GULF OF CARPENTARIA, AUSTRALIA

The race was barely nine minutes old when Jason Chaser lost his steering rudder.

At 430 miles an hour.

The worst thing was, it wasn't even his fault. Some crazy kid from North Korea driving a homemade hunk-of-junk swamp-runner had lost control of his car while trying to pull an impossible 9-G turn and had crashed spectacularly into the crocodile-infested marshes right in front of Jason, sending sizzling pieces of his car flying in every direction—three of which punched *right through* Jason's tailfin like a volley

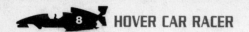

of red-hot mini-meteorites, rendering his steering vanes use-
less.

Jason jammed back on his collective, and somehow
managed to right the *Argonaut* with only his pedal-
thrusters just as—*shoom!-shoom!-shoom!*—three of the
other top contenders whizzed by, rocketing off into the
distance, kicking up geyser sprays in their wakes.

The *Argonaut* slowed to a complete stop, hovering
three feet above one of the thousands of water-alleys in
the vast swamp at the edge of the Gulf of Carpentaria.

The Bug's voice came in through Jason's earpiece. The
Bug was Jason's navigator, co-driver, and little brother. He
sat in the back of the *Argonaut*'s cockpit, slightly above
and behind Jason.

Jason bit his lip as the Bug spoke.

Then he shook his head determinedly. "No way, Bug. I
didn't come here to bow out in the first ten minutes. We're
not out of this yet. You just plot our course. I'll do the rest."

And with that he gunned the thrusters, flinging the *Argonaut* back into the race.

When they had arrived in Pit Lane earlier that morning, Jason and the Bug had sensed an unusual level of excitement in the air.

It was a good crowd—80,000 bustling spectators taking their places in the giant hover-grandstands overlooking the Gulf.

Of course, this was nothing like the crowds they got at the pro events. There, anything less than a million spectators was seen as a poor showing.

Part of the excitement stemmed from the fact that this year there were five drivers, including Jason, who were in contention to take out the regional championships and thus garner a precious invitation to the International Race School, gateway to the professional circuit.

But it was in Pit Lane itself that the excitement was at its highest.

Everyone was whispering and pointing at the two distinguished-looking gentlemen being shown around the VIP tent by Randolph Hardy, the portly president of the Indo-Pacific Regional Directorate of the IHCRA, the International Hover Car Racing Association.

Whispered voices:

"Gosh, it's LeClerq! The dean of the Race School . . ."

". . . other one looks like Scott Syracuse, the guy who was in that accident in New York a couple of years ago and almost died . . ."

"Someone was saying they're here to scout for *extra* candidates for the Race School . . ."

"No way . . ."

Jason eyed the two visitors strolling through the VIP tent with Randolph Hardy.

The older man was indeed Jean-Pierre LeClerq, principal

of the International Race School, the most prestigious racing school in the world.

Located in Tasmania—an enormous island at the bottom of Australia that was wholly owned by the Race School—it was more a *qualifying* school than a strictly teaching institution. While lessons were certainly taught there, it was your ranking in the School Championship Standings that really mattered. It was that ranking that got you a contract with a pro-racing team after your year at "the School." Not surprisingly, the Race School had produced nearly half of the drivers currently on the pro circuit.

LeClerq was a regal-looking fellow, with a perfectly groomed mane of white hair and an imperious bearing. His suit looked expensive. Jason figured it probably cost more than his entire car did.

The man beside LeClerq was far younger, in his early thirties. He was sort of handsome, with intense features and impenetrable black eyes. He also walked with a cane and looked like he'd rather be at the dentist having root canal therapy than be here at the Indo-Pacific Regional Championships.

Jason recognized him instantly. He had the man's trading card in his bedroom back home.

He was Scott J. Syracuse, otherwise known as "The Scythe," one of the best racers ever to have helmed a hover car . . . until he busted the neurotransmitters in his brain in a horrific crash at the New York Masters three years ago. These days, modern medicine could fix just about any broken bone in your body, even a busted spine, but the one thing man hadn't figured out was how to fix the human brain. If you busted your brain, your racing career was over, as the Scythe had found out.

Just then Syracuse turned and his ice-cool eyes locked on Jason.

Jason froze, caught staring.

A full second too late, he looked away.

Truth be told, he actually felt embarrassed under Syracuse's glare. All the other drivers here wore coordinated outfits that matched the color schemes of their cars. Some even had the new Shoei helmets. Others still had full pit crews wearing their team's colors. Jason and the Bug, on the other hand, wore denim overalls and their dusty farmboots. They raced in old motorcycle helmets.

Jason scowled. He could hide his eyes, but he couldn't hide his clothes.

He also couldn't hide his hover car from Syracuse's level gaze. But that was another story.

The *Argonaut*.

Car No. 55.

It was Jason's pride and joy, and he spent every spare minute he had working on it. It was an old Ferrari Pro F1 conversion that he'd found in a junkyard four years ago—one of those early hover cars converted from old Formula One cars.

It had the bullet-shaped body of an old F1 car, complete with nosewing, hunchbacked fuselage, and wide tail rudder, but with the added features of a navigator's seat tucked immediately behind the driver's cockpit and a pair of swept-back wings stretching out from its flanks.

Most incongruously for an old F1 car, however, it had no wheels. Hover technology—the six shiny silver discs on its underbelly called *magneto drives*—had made wheels unnecessary.

While he liked to think otherwise, Jason knew it wasn't a real Ferrari Pro F1. Only the chassis. The rest of it was a hodgepodge of machinery and spare parts that Jason had scrounged from farm vehicles and the local wrecker's yard. Even its six race-quality magneto drives—a mix of GM, Boeing, and BMW mags—were secondhand.

Despite its eclectic innards, the *Argonaut*'s exterior was beautiful—it was painted blue white and silver in a way that accentuated the car's fighter jet–like shape.

Jason himself was fourteen years old, blond-haired, blue-eyed, and determined. At school, he was good at math, geography, and game theory. He wore his sandy-blond hair in a messy "Mohican" style reminiscent of the retired English footballer, David Beckham.

At fourteen, he was also rather young to be at the Regional Championships. Most of the other drivers at this level of racing were seventeen or eighteen. But Jason had finished in the top three in his district trials, just like the rest of them, which meant he had as much right to be here as they did.

With him as his navigator was the Bug—his brother, and at twelve, even younger. With his tiny body and his big thick-lensed glasses, the Bug confounded a lot of people. He didn't talk much. In fact, the only people he would speak to were Jason and their mother, and even then only in a whisper. Some of the doctors said that the Bug was borderline autistic—it explained his excessive shyness and social awkwardness while also explaining his mathematical genius. The Bug could tell you what 653 × 354 was . . . in two seconds.

Which made him the perfect navigator in a hover car race.

The Carpentaria Race was a "gate race."

The most famous gate race in the world was the London Underground Run—a fiendishly complex race through the tunnels of the London Underground—and the Carpentaria Race was based on the same principle.

Instead of doing laps around a track, a gate race had no actual track at all. Rather, it took place over a wide area of open terrain 400 miles wide by 400 miles long. In today's case, that terrain was the vast swampland on the edge of Australia's Gulf of Carpentaria: a marshy landscape that featured a labyrinthine network of narrow waterways cutting through the swamp's eight-foot-high reed fields and the high coastal sandbars of the Gulf itself.

Positioned at various points around this maze of natural canals were approximately 250 bridgelike arches through which the racers drove their hover cars. As your car whizzed through a gate arch, an electronic tag attached to your nosewing recorded the pass.

Passing through a gate gave you points. Gates farther away from the Start-Finish Line were worth more; those that were closer, less. The farthest gate from the Start-Finish Line, for example, was worth 100 points. The nearest, 10 points.

The trick was: there was a strict time limit.

You had three hours to race through as many gates as you could, *and then get back to the Start-Finish Line*.

This final element was crucial.

Every *second* that you were late coming back cost you *one point*. So coming home just a minute over the three-hour mark would cost you a massive 60 points.

The driver with the most points won.

Which made it a tactical race in which navigators played a key role.

No driver, no matter how skilled or fast, could get through all the gates in the allotted time—which meant *choosing* which gates to go for within that time limit. And since computer navigation programs were strictly forbidden at all levels of hover car racing, having a good navigator made all the difference.

Add to that pit stops—magneto drives overheated, coolant tanks needed to be refilled, compressed-air thrusters had to be replaced—and the many other vagaries of racing, and you had a serious strategy contest on your hands.

The *Argonaut* screamed across the marshland, rushing through a narrow alleyway flanked by walls of eight-foot-high reeds, kicking up a whitewash of skanky swampwater behind it.

380 mph . . . 385 . . . 390 . . .

With his steering fins flapping uselessly inside his broken rear spoiler, Jason steered with his two rear thrusters instead—alternating left and right, incredibly using his pedals to control the speeding bullet that was his hover car.

The Bug had plotted their course well. Every trip to the pits allowed Jason to see the big electronic scoreboard mounted above the main grandstand, with its up-to-the-second tally of all the racers' accumulated scores so far:

	DRIVER	NO.	CAR	POINTS
1.	BECKER, B.	09	*Devil's Chariot*	1,110
2.	RICHARDS, J.	24	*Stormbreaker*	1,090
3.	TADZIC, E.	19	*San Antonio*	1,010
4.	YU, E.	888	*Lantern-IV*	1,000
5.	CHASER, J.	55	*Argonaut*	990

The accident had hurt them.

Lost them a lot of time. And no matter how hard Jason tried—and he tried as hard as he could—steering with his feet just wasn't as good as steering with his hands.

And with each trip to the pits, he could see the *Argonaut* falling farther and farther behind the leaders, dropping down the scoreboard.

What made it a hundred times worse was the identity of the driver who was leading: Barnaby Becker, a senior from Jason's school back home in Halls Creek.

Becker was eighteen, red-haired, freckled, cocky, and rich. His father, Barnaby Becker Sr., was a businessman who owned half of Halls Creek.

Mr. Becker had bought his son one of the best production hover cars money could buy—a beautiful Lockheed-Martin ProRacer-5. He had also once employed Jason's dad, a fact that Barnaby—a nasty kid if ever there was one—never failed to remind Jason of.

Nevertheless, Jason flew on, right to the end, zinging

through as many arches as the broken but valiant *Argonaut* could manage, following the Bug's revised course.

It didn't matter.

As the giant clock above the Start-Finish Line ticked over from 2:59:59 to 3:00:00, and the last hover cars shot across the line to the cheers of the 80,000-strong crowd, the *Argonaut*, piloted by Chaser, J., was at the bottom of the scoreboard.

Jason pulled his beloved car to a halt in his pit bay and dropped his head.

In the most important race of his life—in front of 80,000 people; in front of the most distinguished pair of spectators he would ever race in front of—Jason Chaser had come in stone-cold last.

The world was changed forever with the invention of the hover car.

Indeed, over the course of human history, few inventions could claim such an instantaneous and immediate global impact.

Gutenberg's printing press, Nobel's dynamite, the Wright brothers' flying machine—sure they were all impressive, but their impact on the world paled in comparison to the global *revolution* that was brought about by Wilfred P. Wilmington's hover car.

Much of the fuss had to do with the eighty-year-old Wilmington's extraordinary decision to make his amazing new piece of technology freely available to anyone who wanted to exploit it.

He didn't patent it. He didn't sell it to a major corporation. Not even a special delegation led by the President of the United States himself could convince him to keep the technology solely for the benefit of the U.S.

No. Wilfred P. Wilmington, the eccentric backyard inventor who claimed that he had more than enough money to live out his twilight years in relative comfort, did the most extraordinary and unpredictable thing of all: He gave his technology to the world for free.

The response was immediate.

Since hover technology required no gasoline to fuel it, the oil-producing countries of the Middle East crumbled. Oil became meaningless, and the United States—the world's largest consumer of oil—canceled all its Mideast contracts. The fortunes of the Saudis and the Sultan of Brunei went up in smoke in the blink of an eye.

Car companies embraced the new technology and—aided by their already-existent factories and mass-production assembly lines—they pumped out hover cars by the million. The first Model-T/H (for "Hover") Ford rolled off the Ford Motor Company's production line barely one year after Wilmington's incredible announcement. BMW, Renault, and Porsche followed soon after.

They were quickly joined, however, by an unlikely set of competitors: airplane manufacturers. Lockheed-Martin, Airbus, and Boeing all began to produce family-sized hover vehicles too.

Overland travel became faster—New York to L.A. now took ninety minutes by car. Seaborne cargo freighters crossed the world's oceans in hours not days.

The world became smaller.

Professor Wilmington had originally named his discovery an "electromagnetically elevated omni-directional vehicle," but the world gave it a simpler name: the hover car.

The technology underpinning the hover car was disarmingly simple and wonderfully universal.

Every moment of every day, upwardly moving magnetic waves radiate outward from the Earth's core. What Wilmington did was create a device—the "magneto drive"—that *repelled* this upwardly-moving magnetic force. And while scientists marveled at Wilmington's clever fusion of ferromagnetic materials and high-end superconductors, the general public reveled in the result.

For the result was perpetual hover.

As long as the world kept turning, hover cars could retain their lift. And so the public's greatest fear about hover technology—cars dropping out of the sky—had been assuaged.

Hover technology spread.

Passenger cars and hover buses filled cities. Cargo freighters zoomed across the seas. Children's hover scooters

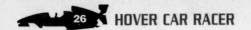

became all the rage. And of course the world's military forces found their own uses for the new technology.

But the advent of any new type of travel technology—boats, cars, planes—always brings forth a certain kind of individual and the hover car would be no exception to this rule.

Soon after the spectacular arrival of this new form of human movement came the arrival of a new kind of person: part race-car driver, part fighter pilot, all superstar.

The hover car racer.

The official presentation of prizes was enough to make Jason puke.

High on the podium, Barnaby Becker stood smugly between Regional Director Hardy and the principal of the International Race School, Jean-Pierre LeClerq.

Smiling for the cameras, LeClerq handed Barnaby the winner's trophy, a gigantic bottle of Moët champagne, and a check for a thousand dollars.

Jason did notice, however, that Principal LeClerq's sidekick, the ex-racer Scott Syracuse, was not on the stage. In fact, Syracuse was nowhere to be seen.

LeClerq shook Barnaby's hand, then he took the mike.

"Ladies and gentlemen," he said. "This being the end of the regional season, I have another presentation to make. With his victory today, young Master Becker has topped the local competition standings, and as such, has won for himself another prize: He has won an invitation to study at the International Race School. Master Becker, it would be our honor to have you as a student next year."

With that, LeClerq handed Barnaby the famous gold-edged envelope that every young racer dreamed of receiving.

The crowd roared their approval.

Barnaby took the envelope, thanked LeClerq, and then he punched the air with his fist and popped the cork on his champagne bottle and the festivities began.

Watching from Pit Lane, Jason just stared at the scene with his mouth agape, devastated.

Beside him, the Bug shook his head. He whispered something in Jason's ear.

Jason snuffed a laugh. "Thanks, man. Unfortunately, you're not the principal of the Race School."

Then he spun on his heel and went back to their pit bay to load up the *Argonaut*.

The Bug scurried after him.

When they got back to their bay, they were surprised to find that someone was already there.

Scott Syracuse was standing in the doorway to their pit bay. He was leaning inside it, peering up at the *Argonaut*'s damaged tail section.

"Er . . . hi there. Can I help you?" Jason said.

Syracuse turned, leaning on his cane. He leveled his cool gaze at Jason. "Master Chaser, isn't it?"

"Yes."

"An appropriate name for you based on today's effort, don't you think? Scott Syracuse. I'm here with Professor LeClerq. I teach with him at the Race School."

"I know who you are, sir. I have your trading card." Jason felt stupid as soon as he said it.

Syracuse nodded at the *Argonaut*. "Your steering rudder's broken."

"Yeah. I got hit by some debris from that crazy kid who tried to pull a 9-G banking turn."

"When did that happen?"

"About nine minutes in."

Syracuse stopped, turned abruptly.

"Nine minutes in? So how did you steer after that? Thrusters?"

"Yep."

"Let me get this straight. You lost your steering nine minutes into the race. But you continued on anyway, steering with your *pedals* instead of your steering wheel."

"That's right, sir."

Syracuse nodded slowly. "I wondered . . ."

Then he looked directly at Jason. "I've got another

question for you. You started the race differently than everyone else—you headed out for the gates on the western side of the course while most of the others went northeast. Then you got hit and changed your race plan."

Syracuse pulled a map of the course from his back pocket. On it were little markers depicting all 250 gates on the course.

"Can you tell me what your original plan was?"

Jason swapped a glance with the Bug. "What do you say, Bug?"

The Bug nodded—eyeing Syracuse warily.

Jason said, "My little brother here does our navigating. He's the guy who plotted our course today. We call him the Bug."

Syracuse offered the map for the Bug to take.

The Bug stepped behind Jason.

Jason took the map instead. "He's a little shy with people he doesn't know."

Jason handed the map to his brother, who then quickly—and expertly—drew their race plan on it. He handed the map back to Jason who passed it on to Syracuse.

Syracuse stared at the map for a long moment. Then he did a strange thing. He pulled out *another* map of the course, and compared the two. Jason saw that this other map also had markings on it, showing someone else's race plan.

At last, Syracuse looked up, and gazed closely at Jason and the Bug, as if he were assessing them very, very carefully.

He held up their race plan.

"May I keep this?"

"Sure," Jason shrugged.

Scott Syracuse pursed his lips. "Jason Chaser, hover car racer. It's got a nice ring to it. Farewell to you both."

★ ★ ★

Jason and the Bug arrived back home in Halls Creek around seven that evening, with the *Argonaut* strapped to a trailer behind their dusty old Toyota hover-wagon.

Halls Creek was a little desert town in the far northern reaches of Western Australia. The exact middle of nowhere, Jason liked to say.

The lights were on in the farmhouse when they arrived, and dinner was on the table when they walked in.

"Oh, my boys! My boys!" Martha Chaser cried, running to the door to greet them. "Jason! We saw it all on the television: that silly boy who crashed right in front of you! Are you both all right?"

She swept the Bug up into her arms, engulfing him in her wide, apron-covered frame. "You didn't hurt my little Doodlebug, did you?"

The Bug almost disappeared in her embrace. He seemed very content in her arms.

"He's okay," Jason said, taking a seat at the table. "Only thing he suffered was the humiliation of coming dead last in front of Jean-Pierre LeClerq."

"Who?"

"Never mind, Mom."

Just then, their father, Henry Chaser, came into the kitchen, his overalls caked with dust from a day's work on the farm.

"Well, hey there! The racers return! Good racing today, sons. Tough call with that kid who banged up your tail."

"Friggin' idiot mangled our steering," Jason groaned as he wolfed down some mashed potatoes. "Wrong place, wrong time, I guess."

"Oh, no," Henry said, smiling. "No, no, no, no. *You* lost your steering, Jason. You *put yourself* in the wrong place at the wrong time."

"Now, Henry, leave them be . . ." Martha rolled her eyes. Her husband was a hover car racing enthusiast. He

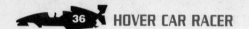

watched it on the television all the time, loved to analyze it—the classic couch coach. It was he who had introduced the boys to mini-cart racing in the back paddock at the ages of five and three.

Jason took the bait. "No way, Dad! I didn't put myself in the wrong place. It was just plain bad luck . . ."

"No it wasn't," Henry said. "It was *racing*. I think this was a good lesson for you both. Racing not only involves beating the other top contenders—it also involves *avoiding* those who *aren't* as talented as you are.

"Sometimes racing isn't fair, Jason. Sometimes you can do everything right in a race and *still* not win. I remember once in the Sydney Classic, the leader was ahead by two whole laps and then he got sideswiped by a tail-ender coming out of the pits. Just like that, he was out of the race—"

The doorbell rang.

Henry Chaser got up, didn't stop talking. ". . . Guy was way out in front and he just got *nailed* by this stupid rookie. God, what was his name? Heck of a driver, he was. Young fella. Got wiped out a couple of years ago. Ah, that's it, it was . . ."

He opened the door. And remembered. He turned back inside. ". . . Syracuse! That's who it was. Scott Syracuse."

He turned to face their visitor.

Scott Syracuse stood in the doorway. Tall and formal.

Henry Chaser almost swallowed his own tongue.

"Oh. My. Goodness," Henry stammered. "You're . . . you're . . ."

"Good evening, sir. My name's Scott Syracuse. I met your sons at the race today."

"Ah . . . ye—yes," Henry Chaser said.

Jason stood up. "Mr. Syracuse? What are you doing here?"

Syracuse remained in the doorway. "I came to ask you a question, young Master Chaser. Oh, and your brother, too."

"Yeah . . ."

"I was rather taken with the way you drove today, Master Chaser. With your feet and with your heart. I believe that with the proper training, your skills could be sculpted into something very special. I also ran your little brother's race plan through a professional course-plotting program on a computer. His race plan was 97 percent efficient. Almost the optimal plan for that course. But you guys didn't receive the gate layout until two minutes before race time. Your little brother formulated that race plan in the space of two minutes *in his head*. That's impressive.

"In short, I think you two make quite a team. Nobody else caught my eye today, but you two did. And now that I work at the Race School in Tasmania . . ."

Jason felt his heart beating faster. "Yes . . ."

"Master Chaser," Syracuse said. "Would you and your brother like to come and study at the International Race School under my supervision?"

Jason's eyes opened wide.

He spun to face his mother. Her eyes were tearing up.

He looked at his dad. His mouth had fallen open.

He turned to the Bug. The Bug's face was a mask. He slowly kicked back his chair and came over to Jason, stood on his tiptoes and whispered something in Jason's ear.

Jason smiled.

"What did he say?" Syracuse asked.

Jason said, "He says your race computer must be broken. His race plan was perfect. Then he said, 'When do we leave?'"

PART II

RACE SCHOOL

THE INTERNATIONAL RACE SCHOOL
HOBART, TASMANIA

Dangling off the bottom of Australia is a large island shaped like an upside-down triangle.

Once known by the far more intimidating name of Van Diemen's Land, it is now simply called Tasmania.

It is a rugged land, tough and forbidding. It features jagged coastal cliffs, ancient rain forests, and a winding network of long, open highways. Dotted around its many peninsulas are the grim sandstone remains of British prisons built in the nineteenth century—Port Arthur, Sarah

Island. Names you didn't want to hear if you were a nineteenth-century criminal.

Once Tasmania was the end of the world. Now, it was just a pleasant two-hour hover liner cruise from Sydney.

Jason Chaser stood on the deck of the liner as it sailed up the Derwent River, and beheld modern Hobart.

With its elegant mix of the very old and the very new, Hobart had become one of the world's hippest cities. Two-hundred-year-old sandstone warehouses blended beautifully with modern silver-and-glass skyscrapers and swooping titanium bridges over the river.

Through a quirk of fate, the entire island was owned by the International Race School, making it the single largest privately owned plot of land in the world.

Back in the early 2000s, the Australian state of Tasmania had been in decline, its population both aging and dwindling. When the population fell below 50,000 people, the Australian government took the extraordinary

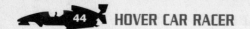

step of privatizing the entire island. Tasmania was bought by an oil-and-gas company that never saw hover technology coming. In the liquidator's sale of the dead company's assets, the island-state was bought by Phillip T. Youngman, the leader of a strange group of people who planned to create a school for the nascent sport of hover car racing.

The rest, as they say, was history.

As desert boys, Jason and the Bug had never seen anything like the East Coast of Australia.

Their cruise liner had swept past Sydney on its way to Tasmania. Just off Sydney, stretching down the Pacific coastline, they'd seen the famous Eight Dams—a simply amazing feat of mass-scale construction. A few years ago, engineers had literally held back the Pacific Ocean while they built eight massive hydroelectric dams a few miles out from the coast.

The eight waterfalls that now streamed majestically down the faces of the dams provided an endless supply of clean power with an added bonus: The waterfalls were the second most-visited tourist attraction in the world behind the Pyramids, and a spectacular backdrop to the annual hover car race held in Sydney—the Sydney Classic—one of the four Grand Slam races.

The cruise liner pulled into the dock at Hobart.

Jason and the Bug grabbed their bags and made for the gangway bridge—

—where they were cut off by two surly youths.

"Well, if it isn't little Jason Chaser again," Barnaby Becker sneered, blocking their way. At eighteen, Becker was a full head and shoulders taller than Jason. He was also now the Indo-Pacific Regional Champion, a title that garnered some respect in racing circles.

Barnaby nodded to his navigator: Guido Moralez, also

eighteen, with shifty eyes and a slick sleazy manner.

"I dunno, Guido," Barnaby said. "Tell me how a little runt who comes stone *motherless* last in the regionals gets to come to Race School."

"Couldn't tell ya, Barn," Guido said smoothly, eyeing Jason and the Bug sideways. "But I hope they're up for it. You never know what sort of accidents can happen in a place like this."

This exchange pretty much summed up their trip.

After their unexpected invitation to come to Race School, Jason and the Bug hadn't seen Scott Syracuse. He was taking a private hover plane to Tasmania, and had said he would meet the boys there. Unfortunately, this meant Jason and the Bug—already outsiders on account of their ages—had had to endure the taunts of Becker and Guido all the way to Tasmania.

Barnaby, knowing that Jason and the Bug lived with adoptive parents back at Halls Creek, took particular joy in including the word *motherless* in most of his snide remarks.

The Bug whispered something in Jason's ear.

"What! What did you say?" Barnaby demanded. "What's with all this whispering, you little moron? Why don't you talk like a man?"

The Bug just stared up at him blankly.

"I asked you a question, punk—" Barnaby moved to grab the Bug by his shirt, but Jason slapped the bigger boy's hand away.

Barnaby froze.

Jason didn't back down, returned his gaze.

"Ooh, I smell *tension*." Guido Moralez rubbed his hands together.

"Don't you touch him," Jason said. "He talks. He just doesn't talk to people like you."

Barnaby lifted his hand away, smiled. "So what did he say, then?"

Jason said, "He said: 'We ain't motherless.'"

The Race School was situated directly opposite the dock, on the other side of the wide Derwent River, inside a shimmering glass-and-steel building that looked like a giant sail.

Jason and the other new racers were led into the school's cavernous entry foyer. Famous hover cars hung from the ceiling: Wilmington's original prototype, the H-1, took pride of place in the center, where it was flanked by Ferragamo's Masters-winning Boeing Hyper-Drive and an arched gate from the London Underground Run.

"This way," their guide said, leading them into a high-tech theater that looked like Mission Control at NASA.

An enormous display screen up front faced fifteen rows of amphitheater-like seating. Each seat was fitted with a computer screen. A gallery at the very back of the theater was provided for the media and at the moment it was full to bursting.

"Welcome to the Race Briefing Room," the guide said. "My name is Stanislaus Calder and I am the Race Director here at the school. Trust me, all of you drivers will come to know this room very well. Please take a seat. Professor LeClerq and the teaching staff will be joining us shortly."

Jason looked around the room, checking out the other racers.

There were about twenty-five drivers in total, most of them older boys of seventeen or eighteen. Nearly all of them sat with two companions: their navigators and mech chiefs. Jason and the Bug didn't have a mech chief, having always done their own pit work. Syracuse had said they would be matched up with someone upon the start of classes.

Jason saw Barnaby Becker and Guido sitting up the back with some other older boys. A few girls were scattered about the room, most of them wearing the black coveralls of mech chiefs, but the assembled crowd was largely male.

One girl, however, caught Jason's eye. She was very pretty, with an elfish face, bright green eyes, and strawberry-blonde hair. She looked about seventeen and sat all by herself way over at the right-hand end of the front row.

It took Jason a moment to realize that not a few of the reporters in the media gallery were gazing directly at her, pointing, trying to get photos of her. Jason didn't know why.

"Close your mouth and stop drooling," a husky female voice said from somewhere nearby.

Jason turned to find the girl seated immediately behind

him also staring at the pretty girl in the front row. "Ariel Piper is way outta your league, little man."

"I wasn't looking at her like *that*," Jason protested.

"Sure you weren't." The girl behind him was about sixteen, with a round face, bright flame-orange hair (with matching flame-orange horn-rimmed glasses) and a wide rosy-cheeked grin. "I'm Sally McDuff, mech chief and all-round great gal from Glasgow, Scotland."

"Jason Chaser, and this here's the Bug. He's my little brother and my navigator."

Sally McDuff assessed the Bug for a long moment. "The Bug, huh? Well aren't you just the *cutest* thing. How old are you, little one?"

The Bug went pink with embarrassment.

"He's twelve," Jason said.

"Twelve . . . ," Sally McDuff mused. "Must be some kind of mathematical whiz if someone invited him here. Nice to meet you, Jason Chaser and his navigator, the Bug.

I imagine we'll be running into each other again over the course of this year. Hope you get a good mentor."

"What do you mean?"

"Gosh, you are a newbie. Getting through Race School ain't just about being a great racer. Having a top teacher makes a huge difference. Apparently the best is Zoroastro. The Maestro. His students have won the School Championship three out of the last four years. Word is, Charlie Riefenstal is light on homework and heavy on track time, so a lot of drivers want to get him."

"What do you know about Scott Syracuse?" Jason asked.

"Syracuse. Yeah. Teaching full-time this year. I heard he did some fill-in teaching last year when the full-timers went on vacation."

"And . . ."

"Apparently, his students were relieved when their regular mentors got back. They say Syracuse works you long and hard. Lotta theory. Lotta pit practice—over

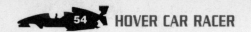

and over until you get it right. And a lot of homework."

"Oh," Jason said.

"Why do you ask?"

"No reason."

At that moment, the rear doors to the theater rumbled open and everyone fell silent. Jean-Pierre LeClerq entered the briefing room, followed by about a dozen teachers and lecturers, all dressed in flight uniforms. Last in the long line of Race School staff, Jason saw Scott Syracuse, limping along with the aid of his cane.

Principal LeClerq took his place behind the lectern on the stage.

"Ladies and gentlemen, sponsors, assembled members of the media, and most importantly . . . *racers*. Welcome to the International Race School. The year has barely begun and yet the world of hover car racing has already seen some great upheavals"—Jason could have sworn LeClerq glanced over at Ariel Piper when he said that—"but here at the Race

School we have adapted accordingly and while the debate has been *vigorous,* we welcome change."

The media photographers clicked away on their digital cameras. Their photos would be on news sites around the world in seconds.

LeClerq continued: "To the new class of candidates, I say this: Welcome. Welcome to the hardest, most demanding year of your lives. Make no mistake, this school is a crucible, a cauldron, a daily trial by fire that will push your skills, your minds—your very characters— to their limits.

"Race School is not for the faint-hearted or the weak-kneed. You will experience the elation of victory . . . and the deflation of loss. You will all partake in the School Championship, while those of you who actually win a race will have the extra privilege of participating in the mid-season Sponsors' Race.

"Some of you will emerge from this crucible forged and

strengthened, and hence worthy of the title 'racer' . . . and from that, worthy of a contract with a professional team. Others among you will not—you will be broken. But take heart, it is no disgrace to withdraw from Race School. Just being invited to come here in the first place means that you are something special.

"Speaking of something special," LeClerq grinned, "I am pleased to announce that we have a surprise for you all today. To give this year's Opening Address we have a very special guest, an alumnus of this school and, let's be frank, a rather famous individual. Ladies and gentlemen, to give the Opening Address, I present to you the best student I ever taught . . . Alessandro Romba, the current World Champion!"

The auditorium came alive.

Heads turned in delighted shock. Murmurs raced across the room. Jason almost fell out of his seat.

At the lectern, Jean-Pierre LeClerq gave a satisfied

smirk—he had sprung his surprise perfectly.

Alessandro Romba was quite simply the most famous man in the world.

La Bomba Romba.

The reigning world champion on the pro circuit, he was the lead driver for the Lockheed-Martin Factory Team. He was also Italian, drop-dead handsome, and perhaps the most daring man to ever helm a hover car: His nickname "La Bomba"—the Bomb—was very well-earned.

He endorsed aftershave lotions, Lockheed-Martin hover cars, and Adidas sportswear. Not a week went by when his face did not appear on the cover of some major magazine or newspaper.

When Alessandro Romba strode out onto the stage from the wings, the entire audience fell into a respectful hush. Not a few women in the crowd primped their hair.

He embraced LeClerq like a son hugging his father, and

then he stood behind the lectern and smiled that million-dollar grin.

The media cameras clicked like machine guns.

Thirty minutes later, La Bomba Romba concluded his speech to roars of approval and a standing ovation.

Jean-Pierre LeClerq retook the lectern.

"Thank you, Alessandro, thank you. It will come as no surprise to any of you that in his year at Race School, Alessandro romped away with the School Championship by a record twenty points. I understand that he will be staying for lunch and is happy to sign autographs too.

"But to some administrative matters: I will now call out each candidate's name and assign them to their mentors. Your mentor will be your teacher here at Race School—as well as your guidance counselor, your confidant, and your surrogate parent. Each mentor will be responsible for three driving teams.

"So. Starting alphabetically. Team Becker, driver Barnaby, you will be under the tutelage of Master Zoroastro. Team Caseman, driver Timothy, Master Raul. Team Chaser, driver Jason, you will be assigned to Master Syracuse: mech chief to be assigned. Freeman, driver Wesley . . ."

Jason turned to the Bug. "Well, little brother. It's time to start Race School."

THE INTERNATIONAL RACE SCHOOL
PIT LANE

Pit Lane pulsed with the noises and smells of racing.

The whirring *hum* of magneto drives. The whine of hover cars screaming down the straightaway. The acrid smell of spent drives and the sweet mintlike odor of green coolant liquid.

After the formalities of the Opening Ceremony were over, it was straight to the racetrack for the new candidates. Their bags were all taken to their dorms, where they would meet them later. Their cars had been unloaded from the liner during the ceremony, and were waiting for them in the pits.

Naturally, Jason and the Bug got lost on the way to Pit Lane.

Race School was a pretty big place, with no fewer than six practice courses and thirteen competition courses, all fanning out from a central pit area on the banks of the Derwent called Race HQ. Finally, they found Pit Lane, with the *Argonaut* sitting inside a bay emblazoned 55.

Scott Syracuse was already there, waiting for them.

"Master Chaser. Master Bug," he said. "So nice of you to join us."

Standing with Syracuse were seven other students— two drivers with their navigators and mech chiefs . . . plus one extra student.

The seventh person was someone Jason recognized.

Sally McDuff.

"Oh, no way . . ." Sally said, seeing Jason and the Bug approaching.

Syracuse said, "You've met already?"

"Yeah, at the Opening Ceremony," Sally said.

Syracuse said, "Well, then, for what it's worth: Jason Chaser, meet Sally McDuff, your mech chief. Ms. McDuff hails from the wilds of Scotland but don't hold that against her. She's a gifted pit technician. For their part, Ms. McDuff, aside from being inexcusably late, the Chaser brothers are quite a driving team."

Jason nodded to Sally.

Syracuse indicated the other two drivers—both were big eighteen-year-olds, one Asian, the other African-American. "This is Horatio Wong and Isaiah Washington. They will also be studying under my tutelage this year."

Both Wong and Washington towered over Jason and the Bug. They eyed them as if they were insects.

"Now," Syracuse said. "Today is Monday. On Wednesday, you will run the first race of the year. Like all

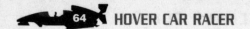

races here at Race School, points will be awarded for the first ten cars on a sliding scale from 10 for the winner down to 1 for tenth place—points that will be tallied for the School Championship.

"During your time here at Race School you will partake in every variety of hover car race: gate races, lap races, sprints, knockout pursuits, and enduros. Wednesday's race is the traditional Race School opener: a supersprint 30-2-1: Last Man Drop-Off. Thirty laps, but every two laps, the last-placed car is removed from the field. It's fast, furious, and unforgiving to racers who fall behind. There are no spectacular comebacks in a Last Man Drop-Off."

Syracuse eyed them all closely, his gaze electric.

"Now, I know a lot of other teachers allow their charges to prepare in relative peace for this first race, using it as a kind of test-the-water, shake-off-the-rust, get-a-feel-for-the-place race. I do not view Race 1 in this way. I view it as a race. A race to be run and hopefully won.

"Nor do I believe in wasting valuable teaching time. Therefore, I will give you all two hours to prep and examine your cars, to make sure they arrived safely, and for those who haven't met to get to know each other.

"We will commence formal lessons in two hours, at 1600 hours, starting with Electromagnetic Physics in Room 17. I have arranged for Professor Kingston, the head of the physics department, to give you all a special private lesson.

"This will be followed by two hours of pit practice commencing at 1730 hours. Dinner begins at 1900, but you can always eat later. As for tomorrow morning's Race Tactics class, I expect that all of you will have read pages 1–35 of Taylor's *The Racing Mind* plus *The Rules of Hover Car Racing,* all of which you will find on your dorm computers. There *will* be a quiz. Any questions?"

The nine students just stared at him in shock.

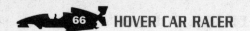

"No?" Syracuse said. "Good. See you in two hours then, in Room 17 for some physics."

Sally McDuff walked in a slow circle around the *Argonaut*, frowning.

She eyed its hunchbacked fuselage, touched its coolant receptacles. "Hmph." Then she dropped to the ground and slid herself under the car, lying on a hoverplank.

Jason and the Bug just watched.

"Hmmm . . ." Sally's voice came from under the car.

She reemerged. Stood up, put her fist to her chin, thinking hard, gazing critically at the glistening blue, white, and silver hover car.

"It's crap," she said, pronouncing the last word in the Scottish manner: *craaap*. "An absolute honest-to-goodness cobbled-together piece of crap. Little Bug, I can't believe a smart guy like you would fly around in this thing. Him," she jerked her chin at Jason, "I could believe, but not you."

The Bug smiled. He liked Sally McDuff.

But she wasn't finished.

"Heck, there must be nine different cars making up this thing. I mean, I can see why she flies fast, but she must be hellishly unstable: you've got the standard six magneto drives along the underbelly of the car, but it's a mix-and-match of three different brands. Luckily, you won't have to worry about that here: the Race School provides us with magneto drives.

"Your Momo directional prism is top quality, but like all the good stuff, Momo prisms wear easily and this one's only got a few races left in it. And what *the heck* did you do to your thrusters, man! Looks like you've been dancing on your pedals! They'll have to be completely stripped, greased, and rebuilt. And you've eaten up your coolant hoses to within an inch of their lives."

"We had a problem with the steering in our last race

back home," Jason said quickly, defensively. "As for the rest, geez, I did build her myself—"

Sally held up her hand. "Easy, tiger. Easy. I wasn't finished. After all that, she's a tough little nut, this *Argonaut*. Looks like you've put her through absolute hell and she's still begging for more. I like tough cars, cars with guts, character, *haggis*. And this car has haggis. Heck, I even like the paint job. And don't you worry, young Chaser. There isn't an engine alive that Sally Anne McDuff can't tune to peak performance."

For the next two hours, Jason and Sally talked (with the Bug speaking through Jason), about their cars and past races, their homes and their dreams involving the racing world.

Sally wanted to be mech chief in a pro team. She was the youngest of nine children and all of the others were boys: all grease monkeys and car freaks. She had spent her early years watching them tinker with their hot rods—but it was only when she got her own car at age fourteen that she revealed the extent of her knowledge: Her own tinkering produced a veritable hover *rocket*. Her father, a stout old Scot named Jock McDuff, was so proud.

Jason told her about himself: living in Halls Creek in far northwestern Australia with his adoptive parents. Martha and Henry Chaser couldn't have children, so for many years they had raised orphans. So far, over the course of forty years, they had raised fourteen parentless kids.

They had found Jason at the local orphanage as a four-year-old. Seated next to him in the playroom had been the Bug, a tiny troublesome boy of two who, they were told, only became quiet when he was with Jason.

When Martha and Henry decided to adopt Jason, they faced an unexpected problem: The four-year-old Jason wouldn't leave the Bug behind. Simply wouldn't leave without him. The dean of the orphanage begged them to take the Bug, too, since there would be no end to the howling if Jason were taken away without him.

And so Martha and Henry Chaser had simply shrugged and decided to adopt the two of them.

Four o'clock came around and they went to their first formal class with Scott Syracuse. It was a killer physics lesson on the workings of magneto drives and the principles behind Wilfred Wilmington's invention and by the end of it, Jason was mentally exhausted.

Which made the ensuing two hours of pit practice absolute torture: over and over again, he would swing the *Argonaut* into their pit bay, bringing it to a halt underneath an enormous spiderlike mechanism called a pit machine.

The pit machine had eight arms, all of which performed different tasks at the same time: magneto drive replacement, coolant refill, compressed-air replenishment, fin realignment—its operation supervised by Sally, the mech chief.

"Clean pit stops are the lifeblood of hover car racing!" Syracuse yelled above the din of his three teams. "Races are won and lost in the pits! Every variety of race contains pit stops—some, like the Italian Run, even require the *pit crew* to travel overland to meet their car at multiple pit areas!

"Pit stops provide races with that crucial element of strategy! *When* should you pit? Should you pit one more time when the finish line is only three laps away? Can you make it round the final lap on only one magneto drive?"

Syracuse smiled. "But before you can formulate pit stop strategies, you have to master the pit stop itself!"

At that moment, as Jason swept into his pit bay underneath the giant claws of his pit machine, he realized—too late—that he'd overshot the pit bay by about twelve inches.

"Chaser! Hold it there!" Syracuse yelled. "Everyone! Freeze! Please observe. Ms. McDuff, initiate the pit machine."

Sally hit the switch.

The pit machine's eight-pronged claws descended around the *Argonaut*—and abruptly stopped, realigned themselves, moved forward a foot, then went about their repair work.

The delay was about five seconds.

"Not good enough, Mr. Chaser!" Syracuse said. "Your pit machine will be loyal to you. But are you being loyal to it by performing a sloppy pit entry? Your competitor just blasted out of the pits four seconds ahead of you and won the race. Imprecision is punished severely in racing. If you are imprecise, *you will lose*. I don't know about you, but I do not race to lose."

Another time, while his pit machine replaced his six undercar magneto drives, Jason—in his eagerness to get away quickly—let the *Argonaut* creep forward over the white line painted on the ground, marking the forward edge of his pit bay area.

There came a shrill electronic scream.

The pit machine immediately withdrew into the ceiling, refusing to work on the car.

"Mr. Chaser!" Syracuse called. "Pit Bay Violation! You just earned yourself a 15-second penalty for illegally creeping out of your pit bay during a stop. Fifteen seconds in a hover car race is an eternity. Again, you lose."

"But—" Jason started.

Syracuse stopped him with an icy glare. "Don't resist your mistakes, Mr. Chaser. Learn from them. To err is human, to make the same mistake twice . . . is stupid."

And with that, mercifully, the pit practice ended.

It was 7:45 P.M.

It was late. Jason and the Bug and Sally were

exhausted. And they still had reading to do for tomorrow.

"Thank you, people," Syracuse said. "I'll see you tomorrow morning."

And he left.

"Could've said, 'Nice work today, kids,'" Jason said.

Sally clapped him on the shoulder. "Nice work today, kid."

"Thanks."

Jason walked to the dining hall, alone. The Bug and Sally had both gone off to their rooms to rest—Jason was going to bring them some food later.

Ahead of him walked Horatio Wong and Isaiah Washington, Scott Syracuse's other two charges. Neither Wong nor Washington even attempted to include Jason in their conversation.

Wong was complaining.

"What is his *problem*? I mean, why should *I* have to attend a stupid *physics* class? As long as my mech chief knows what's happening inside my car, I just want to be left alone to drive it."

"Frickin' A," Washington agreed. "Hey, he pinned me for a pit bay violation. God, everybody does it. When was the last time you saw any racer pinned in a pro race for a pit bay violation? Never! Scott Syracuse wasn't that great a racer when he was driving on the tour anyway. What makes him think he's such a great teacher now?"

Wong lowered his voice, did a Scott Syracuse impression: "*To err is human, to make the same mistake twice is stupid.*"

The two of them laughed.

"Talk about bad luck," Washington said. "Why'd we have to get the demon teacher?"

They came to the dining hall.

All of the other students at the Race School were already well into their dinners, having started at seven. Wong and Washington quickly grabbed a couple of trays and joined a table of boys their age, taking the last available seats.

Jason scanned the room for a place to sit.

Many of the racing teams were eating with their teachers, laughing, smiling, getting to know each other. Syracuse hadn't even offered to dine with his students.

At one table, Jason saw Barnaby Becker and his crew, eating with their teacher, a skeleton-thin man with a beak-like nose.

Jason recognized the teacher instantly: He was Zoroastro, the celebrated former world-champion racer from Russia. One of the very first hover car racers, Zoroastro was still regarded by many as perhaps the most technically *precise* driver ever to grace the pro circuit: he was almost mechanical in his exactness, never missing a turn, just wearing his opponents down until they cracked under the pressure.

Now, as a coach, he was so good—and so vain—that he only deigned to teach two driving teams, not three, as all the other teachers did. And the Race School indulged him.

Which brought Jason's gaze to the other young driver seated with Barnaby and Zoroastro.

He was a strikingly handsome boy of about eighteen. He sat high and proud, and he scanned the dining room as if he owned it. He was dressed completely in black—black racing suit, black boots, black cap—perhaps to match his jet-black hair and deep, dark eyes.

His absolute coolness rattled Jason.

Alone among the racers in the room, his sheer confidence was unsettling. It was said that the very best hover car racers behaved as if they owned the world: You needed a kind of narcissistic superconfidence and self-belief to propel yourself successfully around a track at close to the speed of sound.

Jason made a mental note to keep an eye on this boy in black.

He resumed his search for a place to sit.

A quick survey revealed that there was only one option, and it was a strange one.

Over in the corner of the dining hall, seated at a table all by herself, sat Ariel Piper, the pretty girl he had seen at the Opening Ceremony.

Jason grabbed a tray of food and went over to her table.

As he arrived there, he realized that Ariel Piper was even more beautiful up close. He hoped she didn't see his face flush slightly.

"Hi," he said, "is it okay if I sit here?"

Ariel Piper looked up at him suddenly, as if roused from a daydream, as if she were surprised to hear a human voice so close to her.

"Sure," she said sarcastically, "as long as you're not afraid to catch cooties."

"Come on. I can't catch cooties just from sitting near you," Jason said with absolute honesty. "You only catch cooties from *kissing* a girl—" He cut himself off, blushed bright pink, before adding quickly: "Not that I

came over here hoping to kiss you, miss."

Ariel Piper snuffed a laugh at that, and examined Jason more closely. At seventeen, she was lean and graceful, and way too old for a fourteen-year-old like him. Never had Jason wished more that he was three years older.

Then she said, "You don't know anything about me, do you?"

Jason shrugged. "Nope. Just that you're a student here at the Race School, like the rest of us. I'm Jason Chaser, from Halls Creek, Western Australia."

"Ariel Piper. Mobile, Alabama."

"Why did you say that about catching cooties? Are you sick or something? Is that why you're sitting over here all by yourself?"

Ariel gazed at Jason, a curious smile forming on her pretty face.

"You race with girls back in Halls Creek, Jason?"

"Sure. All the time. Some of the girl racers back home

are the most vicious and dirty—I mean, competitive—racers in the district."

"Okay, then. Have you ever seen a girl racer on the pro circuit?"

That stopped Jason.

"No . . ." he said slowly. "No, I haven't."

Ariel said, "That's because, until now, the Race Schools haven't admitted girls, and since the Race Schools are the prime entry route to the pro circuit, there are no female pro racers. Humankind is funny. We've had all this progress, all these advancements in technology, equality, and equal opportunity, but some prejudices die hard. People still see men and women differently in the world of sport."

"But entry into the school is pretty well set," Jason said. "You either get invited or you get an automatic exemption by winning certain regional championships."

"That's exactly right," Ariel said. "And I won the Southeast-American Regional Championships. After I did, I applied for entry into the International Race School. But the school didn't admit me. They didn't let me in because I was a girl."

"But that's just stupid," Jason said. "If you can race a hover car, it shouldn't matter whether you're a boy or a girl."

Ariel said, "Fortunately for me, Jason, the Australian High Court agreed with you. And they *forced* the school to accept me. It took a fight, but I got in."

And suddenly the light dawned, and Jason understood the presence of all the photographers and journalists at the Opening Ceremony, all focused on Ariel Piper.

He also now understood why she was sitting over here in the corner, all alone, ostracized. And he'd thought that *he* was an outsider because of his age.

"And so now I'm here," Ariel said, "and I'm wondering if it was all worth it. In just one day, my mentor has treated me twice as hard as his male racers. Girl mech chiefs will at least talk to me, but they won't risk eating with me. And forget about the male racers. Then there are all the sideways looks in the corridors and the pit area, the media attention, hell, even the principal doesn't want me here . . ."

She looked away and Jason saw that her eyes were beginning to fill with tears.

"*Hey*," he said firmly. He tried to think of what his mom would say in this situation, and he got it: "No. Don't cry. Don't let them *see you cry*. Then they've won."

That scored.

Ariel raised her head, sniffed once, sucked back the tears.

Jason said, "Ariel, I don't know you that well, but I know this. You're here. Now. At Race School. And the only thing that matters at Race School is this: racing. If you can hold your own on the racecourse, people'll come around."

She turned to face him. "You know, you're pretty smart for a fourteen-year-old."

"I can be a little slow on the uptake," he said, "but just like on the track, I catch up. If it helps, and if you want me to, I'll be your friend while you're here, Ariel."

"I'd like that, Jason. Thanks."

And with that, they started eating together.

THE INTERNATIONAL
RACE SCHOOL:
TASMANIA, AUSTRALIA
RACE 1: SUPERSPRINT 30-2-1

═══ Course

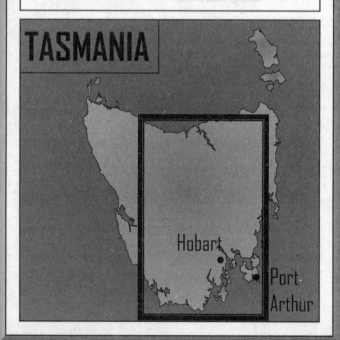

TASMANIA

Hobart

Port
Arthur

RACE SCHOOL, TASMANIA
RACE 1, COURSE 1

Race day.

The roar of hover cars filled the air.

Blurring bullets with racers and navigators inside them whipped past Pit Lane. Large floating grandstands, filled with cheering spectators, enjoyed the carnival atmosphere of the opening race of the Race School season.

Race 1 had been simply electrifying from the start.

A crash on the first corner had seen two cars tumble into the banks of the Derwent River at 310 mph. They'd touched as they'd turned, then flipped and rolled and bounced with frightening speed, shedding pieces of their fuselages as they skimmed the river's surface, before they came to twin thumping halts, their racers (and navigators) safe in their reinforced cockpits and their cars now only good for a trip to the Maintenance and Rebuilding Shed.

Jason had never seen anything like it.

The *pace* of the race was far faster than anything he'd ever been involved in. The intensity was furious. It was the difference between amateur stuff and pro racing.

The race was indeed a "Supersprint 30-2-1: Last Man Drop-Off": 30 laps, and every 2 laps, the last-placed car was removed from the field.

Since there were twenty starters (a few racers had pulled out due to technical problems with their cars), that meant that the last two laps would be fought between six cars.

The course was tight—winding its way westward

through the rain forests of lower Tasmania before returning to Hobart via the treacherous southern coastline of the island.

Such a tight course was brutal on magneto drives, which meant that pit stops would be required every seven or eight laps—creating a (very deliberate) dilemma near the end: Did you pit near Lap 30 or did you try to get to the Finish Line on ever-diminishing magneto drives? Of course, if you were in the pits when everyone else crossed the Start-Finish Line to complete a lap, leaving you the last-placed car, you would be eliminated.

The first two cars eliminated were, naturally, the two that had crashed so spectacularly on the first turn—which meant that the remaining eighteen cars could drive in safety for the next six laps: the third elimination would not occur until the end of Lap 6.

Winding, bending, chasing, racing.

Jason saw the world rush by in a blur: the lush green leaves of the rain forests became streaking green brushstrokes. The sharply twisting road near Russell Falls—one of the great sights of Tasmania—became just another passing point, a spot where you could take someone under brakes.

Sweeping around the coastal cliffs and down the ocean straightaway.

455 mph.

S-bending through a series of silver steel archways that jutted out from the wave-battered southern coastline.

345 mph.

Then braking hard to a bare 130 mph to take the final turn: a wicked left-hand hairpin around Tasman Island, a tall pillarlike rock formation not far from the ruins of the 19th-century prison at Port Arthur.

Then, finally, heading back up to the Derwent River—the home straightaway—hitting top speed: 480 mph.

The *Argonaut* screamed down the straightaway, swept round the deadly Turn 1, and shot into the rain forest.

It was Lap 5, and out of 18 cars, Jason was 10th and feeling pretty good.

Which was precisely when his left-rear magneto drive inexplicably went dead.

Immediately, his car lost some "traction," became harder to handle. Race-spec hover cars customarily have six disc-shaped magneto drives on their undersides. Losing one is bearable, losing two is like driving a wheeled car on a wet road. Losing four is like driving on an ice-skating rink.

Jason's drive console lit up like a Christmas tree.

Sally's voice exploded through his earpiece: "*Jason! You just lost your Number 6 drive!*"

"I know! What happened?"

"*I don't know!*" Sally's voice said. "*According to my telemetry screens, it just packed up and died, lost all power!*"

"Bug!" Jason said quickly. "What do you think? Bring her in?"

The Bug's voice came in through his earpiece.

Jason nodded: "Dang right it'll be close. You sure we can make it?"

The Bug mumbled something.

"Good point," Jason said. "Sally: The Bug's right. We're 10th, a lap-and-a-half away from the next elimination.

Everyone else is probably planning on pitting after Lap 8. If we pit now, we'll go straight to last, but if we can pull a good stop, we'll have a whole lap to catch up. And we'll be on a fresh set of mags. It's our best option."

"*Then come on in, my boys!*" Sally roared. "*This is what it's all about! I'll be waiting!*"

The *Argonaut* took the final Port Arthur hairpin perfectly, and as the leaders shot off down the Derwent on Lap 6, Jason pulled his car into Pit Lane.

He hit his mark perfectly.

The clock started ticking.

00:00

00:01

The pit machine—now christened by Sally as the "Tarantula"—descended on the *Argonaut*, six of its arms removing the car's six underside magneto drives, while its other two arms, respectively, replenished Jason's coolant tank and recharged his compressed-air thrusters.

00:04

00:05

Jason was tapping his foot impatiently. Every second spent in here was a second lost.

Shoom!-shoom!-shoom!

The hover cars that had previously been behind him now whizzed past the pits.

"Come *on!* Come *on!*" he whispered.

00:08

00:09

A ten-second pit stop would be great.

Shoom!

Suddenly the last-placed car shot past the pits. They were now officially last.

The Tarantula was almost done. Only the coolant hose was still connected to the *Argonaut*. Jason, anxious to rejoin the race, leaned forward on his accelerator, creeping forward—

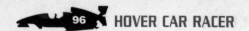

"*Pit Bay Violation! Car 55!*" a shrill amplified voice boomed out from some track-side speakers. "*Fifteen-second penalty!*"

"What!" Jason yelled.

And then he saw the pit bay supervisor—the teachers took turns as supervisor and today it was Professor Zoroastro, Barnaby's mentor and also the mentor of the mysterious boy in black. Right now, he was pointing at the *Argonaut*'s front wings.

They were exactly two inches over the pit bay line.

"Oh, no way!" Jason shouted.

A red boom gate whizzed down in front of the *Argonaut*, preventing it from leaving the pits. A digital timer on the horizontal boom counted down from 00:15.

Now every second seemed an eternity to Jason.

00:10

00:09

00:08

Jason looked over at Sally. Behind her stood Scott Syracuse—his arms firmly folded.

00:02

00:01

00:00

The boom gate lifted and the *Argonaut* shot off the mark, blasting back out onto the course.

The six brand-new magneto drives under him gave Jason a new lease on life.

The *Argonaut* flew like a bullet, gripping the tight turns of the rain forest section as if it were traveling on rails.

With its new mags, it had a grip advantage over the other cars, whose own magneto drives were now nearly six laps old.

Sally's voice: "*You're twenty seconds behind the second-to-last-placed car, Car 70, and gaining. Nineteen . . . now eighteen seconds behind . . .*"

The Bug spoke.

"I know," Jason replied. "I know."

They were gaining roughly one second for every 1¼ miles. But there were only twenty-five miles left to run on this lap.

At this rate—provided Jason raced an almost perfect lap—they'd only catch Car 70 right at the Start-Finish Line.

Whipping past Russell Falls.

Ten seconds behind.

Out round the cliffs, onto the ocean straightaway—just in time to see Car 70 whip around a faraway bluff.

Six seconds.

Weaving through the S-bends of the coastal arches— and suddenly, the tailfin of Car 70 was close.

Four seconds behind.

And then Jason saw the Port Arthur hairpin up ahead, saw the building-sized rock pillar that was Tasman Island.

That was the passing point.

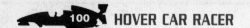

And he had new mags and the other guy didn't.

Car 70 hit the hairpin.

The *Argonaut* took it wider, cutting inside 70's line.

And the two cars rounded the curve together, flying dangerously close to the jagged rocky pillar—

—and the *Argonaut* emerged with its winged nose level with Car 70's bulbous snout!

The crowds on the grandstands leaped to their feet.

The local TV commentators went bananas at the audacity of the move.

Car 70 and the *Argonaut* raced down the Derwent side by side, neck and neck until—*sh-shoom!*—they crossed the Start-Finish Line together.

The official loudspeakers blared:

"*End of Lap 6, eliminated car is Car 70. Racer Walken.*"

The crowd cheered.

Jason floored it—while Car 70 slowed, its driver punching his steering wheel before pulling off into the Exit Lane at the end of the straight.

The *Argonaut* was still in the race.

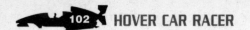

Almost an hour later, Jason was still in it.

In 6th place.

The end of Lap 25 saw the final eight cars enter the pits more or less together.

Jason stopped the *Argonaut* on a dime.

The Tarantula descended, did its stuff.

Entering the pits just in front of Jason had been the boy in black.

His car was a supersleek Lockheed-Martin ProRacer-5, painted entirely in black and simply numbered 1. It was rather presumptuous to number your car *1,* since, in the pro world, that number was allotted to the champion of the previous year. But at Race School, a racer's number was his or her personal choice.

The Black Boy's pit machine worked with extraordinary precision—attaching new mags, filling his car's coolant tanks, pumping in compressed air.

And then suddenly the boy in black was gone,

booming out of the pits a full three seconds ahead of Jason.

It must have been a 7-second pit stop.

How did he do that! Jason thought. *Dang, he's good.*

The Tarantula finished and Jason jammed down on the collective, rejoining the race.

RACETIME: 01:21 HOURS

LAP: 27

Three laps to go. Seven cars left on the track.

The next elimination was the result of a huge crash out on the coastline: the car in 2nd place had lost two mags while wending his way through the S-bends of steel arches—his mags had not been attached properly during his last pit stop and had fallen off.

The result was a 310 mph frontal crash into one of the solid-steel arches. A shocking explosion followed, but the

racer and his navigator had survived by ejecting a nanosecond beforehand.

Which meant that when the field next crossed the Start-Finish line, that driver was eliminated—the fourteenth and last elimination of the race.

So now everyone had pitted three times—as such all were traveling on mags of the same age.

Six cars left. Two laps.

It was now a dash for the Finish Line.

Superfast and supertense. One mistake and you were out. Pressure-driving time.

Place check:

Jason was in 5th place.

The boy in black, in his sleek black Lockheed-Martin, Car No. 1, was first.

Jason could see Barnaby Becker—in his own maroon-colored Lockheed—in 2nd place.

In 3rd, hammering at Barnaby's tail, was a French

youth in a Renault X-700. The French driver was throwing everything at Barnaby, but Barnaby was foiling his every attempt to get past.

In 4th place was a red-and-white Boeing Evercharge-III. This was Ariel Piper's car, No. 16: the *Pied Piper*.

Good for you, Ariel, Jason thought. *Hang in there.*

Then came Jason, followed by Isaiah Washington, in last place.

The six cars took the bend at the end of the straightaway and entered the rain forest for the last time.

Past the falls and out to the ocean straightaway.

Nothing in it.

Then they entered the S-bends of the coastal arches and suddenly, without warning, the *Argonaut* shuddered violently and its tail flailed out wildly behind it like a stunt car in an old movie skidding on a dirt tack and Sally McDuff's voice was blaring in Jason's ear.

"Jason! My telemetry just went berserk! Both of your

rear magneto drives just lost all power!"

Jason grappled with his steering wheel. "I kinda noticed that, Sally!"

Steel archways whistled past him, inches away, just as Washington's car zoomed by, leaving the *Argonaut* in last place.

"Crap!" Jason yelled. "We're screwed! Dang it, we got so far . . ."

They were indeed screwed. With only four mags, Jason couldn't maintain the high levels of speed and control necessary to keep up with the others.

The *Argonaut* fell back. But Jason kept on driving. He was determined to finish the race—and get the 5 points for coming in 6th—even if it meant limping over the line a long way behind the leaders.

He burst out from the S-bends to see the wide-open bay leading to the Port Arthur hairpin.

He saw the all-black Car No. 1 bank into the final turn

with clinical precision, disappearing behind the huge rocky pillar, closely followed by Barnaby—still holding off the French racer in the Renault—and then Ariel Piper swooping in close behind them.

And then it happened.

Ariel's car didn't take the left-hand hairpin.

Instead, it just kept on going straight ahead, shooting out and away to the *right*, heading for the open ocean.

Jason's eyes almost popped out of his head.

"What the—?" he said.

Washington's car took the final turn—pleased now to be moving up into 4th place—and headed for home.

But Jason just kept watching Ariel's hover car.

It was now shuddering violently and listing away to the right—the absolutely wrong direction—shooming off into the distance in a superwide right-hand arc.

"Something's wrong," Jason said. "If she missed the

turn, she would have pulled up by now . . ."

Then came the realization.

"She's lost control of the car."

And as he said those words, Jason saw the final hairpin approaching, and suddenly he had a choice: he could finish the race—and get the 6 championship points for coming in 5th—or he could help Ariel.

The Bug pointed out that the school would send out recovery vehicles to get Ariel.

"No," Jason said. "Look at her. She's too far gone. They won't get to her in time. We're the only ones who can help her."

And with that, he made his decision.

Instead of taking the final left-hand hairpin turn himself, Jason banked the *Argonaut* right, zooming off after Ariel's out-of-control hover car.

The commentators had never seen anything like it.

That the *Pied Piper* had missed the final turn under

intense pressure was nothing new. But that the *Argonaut* had shoomed off into the distance after it was!

Two orange-painted truck-sized recovery vehicles were dispatched from Race HQ—standard practice for a race mishap. They couldn't know that this was no ordinary mishap.

The *Argonaut* zoomed low over the ocean, came alongside the tail of the red-and-white *Pied Piper*, both cars turning in a wide right-bending arc.

"Sally! Get me Ariel's radio frequency!" Jason yelled into his radiomike.

Sally did so, and as the *Argonaut* pulled alongside Ariel's shuddering car, Jason saw Ariel grappling with her steering wheel.

"Ariel! What's wrong?"

"*I've lost power in all my right-side magneto drives, Jason! They all switched off at exactly the same time, just as I was about to take that last hairpin!*"

"What kind of control have you got?" Jason asked.

"*Nothing! It's like everything just cut out at once! Thruster controls are gone! Electronics are unresponsive—I can't even shut down—and my other mags are losing magnetism fast.*"

This was bad. Ariel's left-hand magneto drives were bearing the weight of her whole car, and were thus losing their power twice as fast as they should have been. They were also driving the car in a wide circle, banking right.

What made it worse was the sight looming up ahead.

The southern coastal cliffs of the Port Arthur Peninsula rose up out of the ocean like a gigantic wall. High ocean waves crashed at their feet. Ariel's wide right-bending arc had brought her around a full 270 degrees: she was now rocketing northward, about to crash into the coastal cliffs.

"Ariel! You have to eject!" Jason yelled.

"*No!*" Ariel shouted back.

"No? Are you crazy! Why not?"

"*Jason, if I eject, the* Piper *will smash into those cliffs, and I won't have a car anymore. And without a car, I'll be out of Race School!*"

"And if you die, you'll also be out of Race School!"

"*I am not going to eject!*"

The cliffs were approaching.

Fast. Wide. Immovable.

There couldn't be more than ten seconds to impact.

Jason thought quickly.

"All right . . ." he said.

He gunned his engine and swung the *Argonaut* in underneath Ariel's speeding red-and-white car.

The cliffs rushed toward them.

Nine seconds . . . eight . . . seven . . .

The body of the *Pied Piper* cast a dark shadow over Jason and the Bug, blocking out the sun. Jason saw the underbelly

of the *Piper* less than a foot above his open cockpit.

Six . . . five . . . four . . .

The cliffs were very close now.

Then Jason pulled back on his stick, causing the *Argonaut* to gradually rise . . .

Clunk! The arched hunchback of the *Argonaut* clanged against the underside of the *Pied Piper*. Its wide flat tail-fin also touched the bottom of Ariel's speeding car, providing a kind of three-point stability.

Three seconds . . .

And Jason gunned his thrusters, taking the weight of two hover cars with the engine of one.

The two cars rose together—slowly, painfully—one balancing on top of the other.

Rising . . . rising . . .

Two seconds . . .

Farther . . .

One second . . .

The cliffs were right on top of them now, rushing forward. The *Pied Piper* was going to clear the clifftop, but the *Argonaut*, it seemed, was not.

Too late.

Impact.

The radio aerial on the underside of the *Argonaut* was ripped clean off by the clifftop as Jason rushed over the cliff at astronomical speed.

But they'd made it, clearing the clifftop by inches, pushing Ariel's car over it.

The danger averted, the Race School recovery vehicles swept into position on either side of Ariel's car, capturing her inside a fat beam of electromagnetic energy that extended out between them. The *Pied Piper*'s stability returned immediately and the two recovery vehicles guided it back to Race HQ.

For his part Jason pulled the *Argonaut* away from the

recovery vehicles and returned to Pit Lane.

As they entered the pits, the Bug said something to Jason.

"Shut up, you cheeky little monkey," Jason replied.

The *Argonaut* cruised to a smooth touchdown in its pit bay, where it was met by Sally McDuff, Scott Syracuse, and a crowd of buzzing onlookers.

Sally was smiling broadly.

Syracuse was frowning darkly.

Among the crowd were a phalanx of photographers and local journalists.

"You are one crazy little fella!" Sally roared, yanking Jason bodily from his cockpit and giving him a friendly thump on the helmet. "But mark my words, young man, don't you ever put my little Bug in danger like that again!"

Jason smiled, turned to face Syracuse.

"Congratulations, Mr. Chaser," Syracuse said. "You just made a name for yourself. You also failed to finish the race, which means you lost the 6 championship points that would have gone with 5th place. We'll discuss this later." And with that Syracuse turned and left.

Camera's flashed. The journalists shouldered each other out of the way, shouting their questions, asking Jason what had compelled him to risk his life to save Ariel.

But after the initial frenzy, there came a shout: Ariel Piper had just arrived back in the pits. The media pack dashed off and Jason was left in his pit bay with the Bug and some peace and quiet.

He sat down, caught his breath. The Bug plunked down beside him.

After a few minutes, Sally came over. "I just checked your rear magneto drives on my personal electrometer. Guess what? Those mags were only 10 percent charged when they were attached to the *Argonaut*."

"What?" Jason said. "Only 10 percent? Where did you get them?"

"Same place as everyone else," Sally shook her head. "The School's Parts and Equipment Department. It's where all the cars at the School get their equipment. But wait, there's more."

"Yes . . ."

"You remember that other magneto drive that crapped out on you early in the race and forced you into the pits around Lap 5? Well, I checked it too. It was also undercharged. Same level. Ten percent."

"So what do you think that means?" Jason asked.

"It means," Sally said, "that either we got *galactically* unlucky getting three bogus magneto drives in our allotment . . ."

"Or . . ."

"Or someone set us up," Sally said.

The words hung in the air.

"Someone arranged for us to collect three bogus mags from the Parts Department. Think about it. I picked up eighteen magneto drives for this race, three sets of six. We were going to have to use all of them at some point today. So we were destined to wipe out or at least have an unscheduled pit stop at some stage. Jason," she frowned, "I think someone sabotaged our car today."

A few moments later, Ariel Piper came by their pit bay. The media tornado had got what it needed from her—some sound bites to match their footage—and had gone on its way.

"There he is, my knight in shining armor," she said.

"Hi," Jason said. He introduced Sally and the Bug.

"Thanks for what you did out there," Ariel said. "And for understanding why I couldn't eject."

"Forget about it," Jason said. "You woulda done the same for me."

Ariel shook her head. "I don't know about that, Jason," she said. "For some of us, heroics aren't the natural first instinct. But thanks again."

She stood up to go.

"Oh, and one more thing," she said. "My mech chief, Bonnie, did some quick diagnostics on my car when I got back. Some of my magneto drives had apparently been doctored before the race, drained of 90 percent of their power. And my onboard electronics had also been infected with a time-bomb computer virus that was programmed to go off late in the race—which was why I lost all control on the last turn."

"No way . . ." Jason said. "We got bogus drives, too. But not the other stuff."

Ariel locked eyes with him. "Someone didn't want me to finish this race today. And if it hadn't been for you, it would have been worse—a lot worse. I'm scared, Jason. I think someone wants me out of Race School permanently."

PART III

ENEMIES WITHIN

There was no rest for Jason and his team after the high drama of Race 1.

The races continued—at the rate of two per week, usually held on Tuesday and Thursday, with classes in between.

One thing quickly became clear: the boy in black, the winner of Race 1, was a seriously good racer.

He also won Race 2.

And Race 3.

Jason managed to come in fifth in Race 2, but "DNF'd" Race 3—Did Not Finish—on account of another mysterious mechanical problem, this time a bottle of thinned coolant.

The boy in the all-black Car No. 1 won by a mile on each occasion—and each time he was shadowed by his stablemate, Barnaby Becker. As a result, both of them flew to the top of the Championship Standings, at 30 and 27 points, respectively.

Their mentor Zoroastro strutted around the Race School like a coach with the two top-placed racers in his stable—while behind closed doors other racers complained that Zoroastro's drivers were unfairly driving *as a team*, with Barnaby flying interference for the supercool boy in black.

It took only a few questions for Jason to find out who this mysterious and talented boy in black was.

His name was Xavier Xonora, and it turned out that he was Zoroastro's nephew. Now, not only was he blessed with dashing good looks, great driving skills, an incredible racing pedigree, and a top-of-the-line Lockheed-Martin car, Xavier Xonora also had one other thing going for him.

He was a *prince*.

A solid-gold, bona-fide prince. His parents were the king and queen of the principality of Monesi, a small sovereign European state not far from Monaco.

Whenever he walked by, the mech girls at the Race School tittered and whispered. Every society mother in Hobart begged him to attend their dinner parties, hoping the young prince might take a liking to their dreamy-eyed daughters.

Jason and the Bug would bump into him occasionally in the pits. One time Jason smiled and said, "Hey, Xavier."

The Prince froze in midstride. Turned.

"If you insist on speaking to me, you will address me as *Prince* Xavier or Your Royal Highness," he said, before moving on, nose held high.

"O-*kay*," Jason said after him. "Like that's ever gonna happen."

★ ★ ★

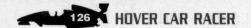

Life at Race School was just nonstop.

Classes, races, homework, and sleep.

For Jason, grappling with the sheer pace of Race School life was difficult.

While he loved the chance to race nearly every other day, no sooner were you finished with one race than you were back in the classroom analyzing it. And then it was straight into the simulator, the race lab, or the pits to practice, practice, practice.

Worse still, for Jason and the Bug a special arrangement had to be made for them to do regular schoolwork in between their racing classes.

It amounted to more information than Jason had ever absorbed in his whole life and at times it was a struggle. While he was certainly smart, he had never been comfortable with the regimented nature of school life. It was all he could do to keep up.

Scattered in among his racing classes were regular

sessions in the school's giant centrifuge—a huge mechanical arm (with a race-car cockpit attached to its outer extremity) that swung in fast sweeping circles. Like the old Dynamic Flight Simulator at NASA, this centrifuge was designed to test each racer's G-force tolerances.

Jason invariably blacked out around 8-Gs, which was the average. Some other racers and navigators could get up to 8.5 or 8.7 before losing consciousness. It was perhaps surprising then when it was discovered that the student who could withstand the most G-forces was . . .

. . . the Bug.

The little guy could withstand an astonishing 9.3-Gs on the centrifuge—and still perform certain physical and mental tasks. And while many of the other students gagged or vomited when they were on the centrifuge, the Bug spent the whole time squealing with delight, like a kid on a roller coaster.

★ ★ ★

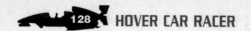

Jason and the Bug were living in their own dorm room in the east wing of the Race School.

It was a high-tech, white-walled, three-level apartment—with recessed bunk beds, auto-foldout sofas, and even a sliding pole to allow quick access between the multiple levels. In effect it was a kid-sized apartment, and as such the best clubhouse in the world. It even had spectacular views of Storm Bay.

Jason loved it, loved the independence of it.

But the Bug was different.

For all his astounding mathematical abilities (and his incredible results on the centrifuge), he was still essentially just a quiet little twelve-year-old from a dusty desert town who missed his mom and his dad.

So late at night Jason would sit with him as they wrote long e-mails home, and when they got a reply several minutes later, the Bug would leap up with delight.

Then they'd sleep and suddenly the alarm clock would be ringing and it would be time for the next race.

And what a variety of races they were.

Gate races, enduros, sprints, and last-man drop-offs, on an equally varied array of courses.

After fifteen races, however, the standings didn't look good for Jason and the *Argonaut* team. It looked like this:

INTERNATIONAL RACE SCHOOL CHAMPIONSHIP STANDINGS AFTER 15 RACES			
DRIVER	**NO.**	**CAR**	**POINTS**
1. XONORA, X.	1	*Speed Razor*	118
2. BECKER, B.	09	*Devil's Chariot*	105
3. KRISHNA, V.	31	*Calcutta-IV*	102
4. WONG, H.	888	*Little Tokyo*	100
5. WASHINGTON, I.	42	*Black Bullet*	99

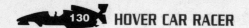

Prince Xavier had won an astonishing five of fifteen races, garnering 10 points for each win. He'd also had strong finishes in the other races, giving him a whopping 118 points out of a possible 150.

Of the twenty-five racers in total, languishing down near the bottom of the standings was:

20. CHASER, J.	55	*Argonaut*	79

After their zero-point efforts for not finishing Races 1 and 3, Jason and the Bug had started the season at the bottom of the standings.

They'd had a couple of podium finishes since—mainly in gate races and the superlong enduros (long-distance races that lasted up to eight hours)—and the points they got for those lifted them slightly in the standings.

But then around Race 9 they were suddenly beset by technical problems again.

After the "depleted magneto drives incident" of Race 1, Sally McDuff had started electrochecking their drives before each race. In Races 9 and 12, she found that they had *again* received depleted mags from the Parts and Equipment Department.

But other technical problems also surfaced.

More thinned coolant in Race 13. A mystery computer virus that occasionally caused the Tarantula to malfunction. It was as if in every race they were fighting against an army of invisible gremlins constantly getting into their systems. If they finished at all, it was only after a huge effort.

So one day, Sally went off to the Parts and Equipment Department to investigate the faulty parts, only to return an hour later, fuming.

"Stupid greasy punk. The desk guy just waved me away," she growled. "Said, 'Sorry, honey, but it wasn't us. You mustn't have taken good enough care of the ones you were given.' Honey? *Honey!* So I told him we got six faulty mags in one race and he just shrugged and stared at me. It was like talking to an Easter Island statue."

Their mentor, Scott Syracuse, offered little sympathy.

It didn't help that their stablemates under Syracuse—Wong and Washington—were in the top five in the standings and performing well in the same races, and experiencing no technical problems at all.

It made Jason appear simply unlucky, or worse, just not good enough.

The beautiful Ariel Piper was having similar problems—with magneto drives and faulty parts. After her near-catastrophic experience in Race 1 caused by a virus in her pit computer, she had installed a new firewall that seemed to have stemmed that problem. She was currently in 12th place—solid but unspectacular for the first girl to attend the Race School.

In any case, a key feature of the school's racing season was fast approaching and it was particularly troubling Jason.

The mid-season Sponsors' Event—a feature race held in front of the school's sponsors, benefactors, and famous ex-students—would be held after Race 25, and it was only open to those students who had *won* a race during the season.

The Sponsors' Event was a huge opportunity to perform in front of some of the major players in the pro racing world. The thing was: Jason hadn't yet won a race, and with fifteen races already down, he was fast running out of races to win.

Either way, it was time to address his team's problems. It was time to go to the source of all the depleted drives, thinned coolants, and faulty parts.

The Race School's Parts and Equipment Department.

The International Race School's Parts and Equipment Department was housed inside a gigantic warehouse behind Pit Lane near the banks of the Derwent River.

It was a colossal structure, so big in fact that the school had built a glorious silver grandstand on top of it, offering a superb view of the main finishing straightaway.

On a rare spare afternoon, Jason, the Bug, and Sally McDuff came to the student entrance and opened it—just as a stocky bull-necked youth with a bristly shaved head emerged from the department.

Sally watched him go with interest.

"Do you know who that was?" she said.

Jason squinted after the bull-necked youth. "No. Who?"

"His name is Oliver Koch. He is Xavier Xonora's mech chief."

"Is that so?"

They entered the Parts Department, came to the service desk that separated visitors from the cavernous interior of the warehouse. The gritty odors of grease, rubber, and coolant pervaded the air.

They were met by a weasel-faced young man named Wernold Smythe. Smythe lazily wiped his grease-covered hands on a rag. He was about twenty-six, laid-back, and creepy.

"Can I help you?" he asked, wedging the rag into one of the low-slung hip pockets on his overalls.

"Yes. I'm Jason Chaser. Team *Argonaut*. We've been having some problems with equipment coming out of the department. Mags that aren't fully powered up, thinned coolant."

"You didn't get faulty mags from here," Smythe said quickly. "Doesn't happen."

"But we did. Our mags were only 10 percent charged."

Smythe leaned forward. "No, *you didn't*. Every mag that goes out of here is electrochecked on the way out." Smythe jerked his chin at Sally McDuff. "Maybe your mech chief screwed up: left 'em too close to a power-drain source, like a portable pit machine generator or a microwave transmitter."

Sally growled. "I'd *never* leave a magneto drive next to a microwave transmi—"

"It's happened before," Smythe shrugged. "As for coolant. We hand it out in the original manufacturer's bottles, with the seals intact. I got some complaints from a couple of other racers—kid from India and that Piper chick. Y'all probably just got a bad batch. In any case, I'll note your complaint."

Just then, the Bug tugged on Jason's sleeve, whispered something in his ear.

Jason nodded—then he glanced at the greasy rag protruding from Smythe's hip pocket.

He said to Smythe: "Would you mind if before our next race my mech chief observes you electrochecking our mags before she takes them away from here?"

Smythe's face turned to ice. "I don't think I like your tone. Are you suggesting something?"

"Like what?"

"Are you suggesting that I'd deliberately allow depleted mags to be given out to certain racers?"

"Let's just say I'm tired of being "unlucky." I just want to ensure that I don't suffer another bout of unluckiness tomorrow."

Smythe said coldly: "I answer to my boss, Department Chief Ralph A. Abbott. He answers to Jean-Pierre LeClerq. How about this: you get me a note from Abbott or LeClerq and I'll let your mech chief observe tomorrow's electrocheck. Until I see that note, why don't you just *piss off* and let me do my job."

His snakelike stare became a fake smile. "Now, unless there's anything else I can do for you, I have to go."

Jason and the others left the Equipment Department.

As they walked away, the Bug whispered in Jason's ear.

"Yeah, I saw it," Jason said.

"Saw what?" Sally asked. "What did the little guy say to you in there?"

"It's not what he said, it's what he saw. The Bug saw something in Smythe's pocket," Jason said. "When we came in, Smythe stuffed his rag into his pocket. But he didn't stuff it in far enough. The Bug saw a wad of hundred-dollar bills sticking out from under it. I can't imagine a grease monkey like Werny Smythe goes to work with that kind of cash on him."

"Which means . . . ?" Sally said.

"Which means he got that money recently. Today. And who was in the Department just ahead of us?"

"Oliver Koch . . ." Sally said.

"That's right. Xavier Xonora's mech chief," Jason said.

The Bug whispered something.

"No," Jason replied. "I don't think we can turn them in yet. Just seeing some money in his pocket isn't enough evidence to prove our case. But I think we're gonna have to keep an eye on Smythe and Prince Xavier's team."

The next day, Jason found himself rocketing north along the eastern coastline of Tasmania in the *Argonaut*, powering through driving rain.

Ducking, weaving, blasting, charging.

He swooped left, banking into a high-speed turn that took him across the midsection of Tasmania.

There was good news and bad news.

The good news: he was coming 3rd in this race, behind Horatio Wong and Isaiah Washington.

The bad news: there were only three cars in the race.

It was a three-man practice race between Jason and the other two students of Scott Syracuse: Wong and Washington.

It was the day before Race 16 and while most of the other teachers had given their students a rest-and-preparation day before the race, Syracuse had arranged for his charges to have a private race of their own on Course 9, a track that circled the lower half of Tasmania.

Despite the atrocious weather, the *Argonaut* was absolutely flying.

It shoomed out over the Serpentine Dam, bending south toward Wreck Bay.

The only problem was, it was almost a quarter of a lap behind the other two racers—thanks to an unexpected malfunction of the Tarantula during its first pit stop. The big pit machine had simply shut down halfway through the stop, meaning that Jason and the Bug had just had to sit helplessly in their cockpit while Sally McDuff frantically rebooted the robot.

The damage was a full quarter lap.

And this was only a 10-lap race.

Being a longer, more open circuit, pit stops were assumed to be necessary every four laps. Or not.

So at the end of Lap 8, Jason had to make the call.

To pit or not to pit?

To not pit—while the other two cars did—would allow him to catch up and even overshoot them. It was a daring move, and something Wong and Washington certainly wouldn't expect.

It was also not altogether unprecedented: some of the greatest come-from-behind wins on the pro circuit had come from drivers who had audaciously skipped their last pit stop.

But the trade-off was lower-powered magneto drives. Could Jason complete the last two laps on ever-diminishing drives? If he drove perfectly—absolutely perfectly—maybe he could.

"Let's do it," he said to the Bug when he turned onto the home straightaway and saw both Wong and

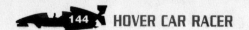

Washington predictably enter the pits.

So Jason gunned it—

—and shot past the entry to Pit Lane.

Wong and Washington both snapped round at the sound of the *Argonaut* booming up the straightaway.

Jason drove hard.

He had two laps to complete and every second he made while the other racers were stopped in the pits was a second he had up his sleeve.

Up the coast he went, then banking left, cutting across the island.

The others finished their pit stops, blasted back out onto the course—in hot pursuit.

Jason urged the *Argonaut* on.

The other two cars closed the gap. But this course wasn't as tight as some of the other tracks and hence wasn't as brutal on magneto drives. Wong and Washington weren't catching up all that quickly.

The Bug told him their magneto drives were down to 15 percent.

"We can make it," Jason replied.

The *Argonaut* hit the western coast, shot down the shoreline. Zoomed round the southern tip of the island, then pointed north and once again saw the home straightaway.

Shoom! It whipped across the Start-Finish Line.

"One lap to go," Jason said.

"*Come on, Jason . . .*" Sally McDuff's voice said in his earpiece.

Wong and Washington's cars blasted across the Start-Finish Line, gaining on Jason like a couple of hungry sharks.

The gap was ten seconds and closing.

Cutting left across the island.

Nine seconds.

The *Argonaut* was becoming very slippery.

Its mags were running at 10 percent, the Bug reported.

"*Jason, conserve your mags! Use your thrusters more!*" Sally said over the radio.

"We're okay!" Jason said. "We've just gotta hold out for half a lap!"

Across the top of the dam. Nose into the rain.

8 percent

He took the left-hander onto the southern coast more gently, losing more time.

4 percent

Wong and Washington were close behind him now—

2 percent

The final stretch was a long "sweeper" round the southern coastal cliffs of Tasmania and not too tough on mags. Jason managed to stay out in front.

Then he hit the final left-hander and . . .

. . . slowed.

0.4 percent . . . 0.2 percent . . . 0.0 percent

"No!" he yelled.

He received no response when he pushed forward on his collective.

Wong and Washington whooshed by the *Argonaut*, rocketing away up the home straightaway, disappearing into the distance, becoming specks.

Wong would cross the line first, winning by 0.3 of a second.

Jason punched his steering wheel. "Dang it!"

He engaged his emergency power reserves to guide the *Argonaut* up the straightaway and limp over the Start-Finish Line, pounded by the pouring rain.

Upon returning to the pits, wet and soaking, he found Wong's team dancing in jubilation. Washington's team was also happy to have finished so strongly.

And Scott Syracuse was just standing there, shaking his head.

"Mr. Chaser. Mr. Chaser. A bold move. But also a *very* stupid one. In over two thousand official hover car races at this school, only ten have ever been won by racers who skipped their last pit stop. That's a success rate of 0.005 percent. It might look audacious when you see Alessandro Romba do it on television but statistically, skipping your last stop is a foolish tactic. Please don't do it again while you are under my tutelage, lest someone think I actually encourage such folly.

"Mr. Wong, good racing. Exceptional pit work on the part of your mech chief. Mr. Washington, your cornering needs work, but you finished well. And Mr. Chaser: You have a lot to do. Work on your tactics and get your mech chief to check your pit machine more closely before each race."

Syracuse turned to leave. "That will be all for today, people. I'll see you tomorrow for Race 16. As usual, be in the pits two hours before racetime. Good night."

And he left.

The next few races passed without any major incidents—no faulty parts or depleted magneto drives.

Just good hard racing.

The *Argonaut* had some promising finishes. A third, then a fifth, which lifted it up in the rankings to 15th.

Ariel Piper caused a minor sensation when she stole victory from Barnaby Becker on the final turn of Race 18. But after that, she was bogged down with technical problems again and in the next three races, she DNF'd twice and fell down in the standings to 14th.

Ariel didn't mind: her win in Race 18 had guaranteed her a start in the much-anticipated Sponsors' Event.

Jason, however, was still winless.

He had come close in Race 22—a gate race around the craters of the old mining town of Queenstown, coming in second behind Xavier Xonora. Again, it had been pouring with unseasonable rain that day—so heavily in fact that several of the gate arches had collapsed in mudslides and the race was nearly canceled.

In the race, however, the Bug had outdone himself, coming up with a very clever race plan that none of the other navigators—not even Xonora's—had even considered.

Jason executed the plan well, but Prince Xavier was an incredible racer—and absolutely awesome in the rain— and his navigator's race plan, while more conventional than the Bug's, was just as effective with Xavier at the wheel, and the Black Prince held on to win the race by a bare point.

Jason kicked himself. Their plan had been superb. Sally's pit work had been great. It was *his* driving that had let them down. He had been the weakest link.

And now they only had three races to get a win.

Another strange thing happened that day.

As Jason stood on the winner's podium with the Bug and Sally, he noticed Barnaby Becker—who had come in 9th—gazing up at him from the crowd, with his and Xavier's mentor, Zoroastro, beside him.

Jason noticed Zoroastro point up at *the Bug* and whisper something to Barnaby.

Barnaby nodded. Only Jason saw the gesture, from way up on the podium. What it meant, at first he didn't know.

That evening he found out. •

As he and the Bug were returning to their dorm from dinner later that night, they found that the lights to their stairwell were not working.

The entire area was dark and silent. Foreboding.

They climbed the stairs, but had only got halfway up when four shadowy figures—two above them, two below—appeared from the shadows.

Trapping them on the stairs.

The two boys above them were Prince Xavier and Barnaby Becker. The two boys below: the stocky Oliver Koch and Barnaby's navigator, the sly Guido Moralez.

Moralez emerged from the darkness.

"Well, well, well, if it isn't the kindergarten class. Good race today, kiddies. Not good enough, but still a sterling effort."

"Thanks . . ." Jason tried to go up the stairs, but Barnaby and Xavier blocked him.

Moralez climbed the stairs, eyeing the Bug. "You little fellas like those gate races, don't you. Like the strategy of them. Like the idea of setting your own course."

"What do you want with us?" Jason said.

"Chaser, Chaser," Moralez said. "That's your problem,

you know, it's always about *you*. But this isn't about you. No. This is about *him*: your little navigator here. I just want to talk with him. Congratulate him on plotting such a great course today. Give him a little prize."

Moralez cracked his knuckles, stood over the Bug. Then he formed a fist, held it in front of the Bug's bespectacled face. "Here's your prize, you little four-eyed freak."

Moralez made to punch the Bug in the face, but Jason rushed forward at the last moment and pushed the Bug out of the way—and in doing so, received the full force of the blow instead.

Jason hit the wall. Hard. Blood spilled from his nose.

"Hoo-ah! Ouch!" Moralez sneered. He moved again toward the Bug, who backed up against the wall, cowering, defenceless, utterly terrified—

"No!" Jason called, standing up on wobbling legs and again moving in front of the Bug. "You don't *touch* him."

The Bug hated to be touched, absolutely *hated* it. Heck, he only let two people in the whole world even hug him: Jason and his mother. He didn't even let his father cuddle him. A full-blown punch from Guido Moralez would probably send him into a catatonic state.

Jason had to do whatever he could to prevent this creep from touching the Bug . . . even if that meant acting as an alternative punching bag.

"You wanna pick on someone," he said to Moralez, "pick on me . . . *loser*."

The bait worked.

"Loser? *Loser!*" Moralez sneered. "You little punk . . ."

Whack! He punched Jason in the gut, the blow sudden and strong. Jason buckled over—winded—but remained standing.

He swallowed.

Raised his head.

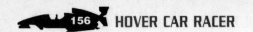

Looked Moralez right in the eye. Baited him again.

"You . . . hit . . . *like a girl*," he said grimly.

Two more lightning-quick blows from Moralez dropped Jason to his knees.

Moralez moved in.

"Enough!" Prince Xavier's voice echoed from the top of the darkened stairwell.

Moralez rubbed his knuckles as he stepped away from Jason. "You forgot what I told you when we arrived here: You never know what kinds of accidents can happen in a place like this. See ya round, Chaser."

Jason just stared up at the silhouette that was Xavier Xonora. "Next time, Xonora," he said, "take us on where it counts. On the track."

The shadow made no reply.

Then as quickly as they had appeared, the bigger boys left, melting away into the darkness, and Jason and the Bug were alone in the stairwell.

The Bug rushed to Jason's side, tears in his eyes, put his arms around his brother.

Jason sat up, touched his nose. "Ow."

The Bug whispered something.

Jason looked at him. "That's okay, little brother. Anytime."

The next morning, in the Race Briefing Room, there came a big surprise.

Accompanying Race Director Calder onto the stage was none other than the principal of the Race School, Jean-Pierre LeClerq. He took the lectern.

"Racers," he began. "I have an announcement to make. Some excellent news has come through. I have just received word from the Professional Racers Association regarding Race School participants in the annual New York Challenger Race."

A buzz filled the room.

The New York Challenger Race was part of the week-long New York Racing Festival, the high point of the hover car racing year, held in October. The climax of the Festival was the New York Masters Series: four different kinds of races, one race per day—a supersprint, a gate race, a multi-car pursuit race, and, last of all, a long-distance quest race. A veritable feast of racing, the New York Masters title was the most prestigious hover car racing title in the world and the last of the four Grand Slams.

The New York Challenger Race, however, was traditionally held two days *before* the Masters series. It was an intricate lap race through a street circuit that traversed the avenues and parks of New York City.

Entry was by invitation only and the race normally featured up-and-coming racers from the satellite leagues. Schools like the International Race School were often given a couple of invitations to disperse as they pleased. Participating in the New York Challenger Race was not just an honor—it was also an incredible opportunity for

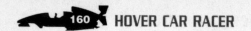

an unknown racer, since it was a chance to race in front of the pro-racing teams who would be assembled in New York for the Masters.

"I am pleased to announce," LeClerq said, "that the Racers Association has allocated the International Race School *four* places in this year's New York Challenger Race!

"In keeping with the school's longstanding tradition in matters such as this, the four invitations to the Challenger Race will be allocated to those racers occupying the top four positions in the Race School Championship Standings at the end of the school competition in September."

The buzzing in the room intensified as racers and their teams quickly conferred, calculating their chances of coming in in the top four.

It was now late May. There was still a long way to go in the School Championships.

Jason, the Bug, and Sally formed a huddle. Jason's face was a little cut and bruised.

Sally whispered: "The top four? Geez, can we make it?"

"There's a lot of racing left in this season," Jason said. "Just about everyone can still make it. Either way, it certainly gives us something huge to race for."

At that moment Principal LeClerq cleared his throat, getting everyone's attention again.

"I also have another announcement to make," he said, "this one concerning the annual Sponsors' Event to be held here at the Race School this coming weekend. Two things. First, the format of the Sponsors' Event."

The format of the Sponsors' Event changed every year: some years it was a gate race, others an enduro, sometimes it was even a series of races.

"This year's Sponsors' Event," LeClerq said, "will take the form of a round-robin tournament: a daylong series of knockout one-on-one pursuit races."

Once again, the room rippled with excitement. Such a
format was similar to a professional tennis tournament:
as you beat one opponent, you proceeded to the next
round, until by the end of the day, only two racers were
left to fight out the final. Every race was do-or-die, which
made for very exciting racing.

But then LeClerq went on. "My second announcement
about the Sponsor's Event is more administrative. As I am
sure you are all aware, the event has long been scheduled
to take place this coming weekend, in front of all of the
school's sponsors and benefactors.

"Owing to the inclement weather of late and its effects
on our courses across the island—mudslides, high seas
along the coasts—it has been decided that Races 23 and 24,
set for today and Tuesday, will be canceled. Weather per-
mitting, Race 25 will go ahead as planned on Thursday."

The announcement made Jason gag. "*What!*" he whispered in disbelief.

But everyone else in the room, it seemed, had been dazzled by the New York Challenger announcement and appeared unfazed by this.

"No *way*," Sally McDuff said. "They just canned two races . . ."

"And we haven't qualified for the Sponsors' Event yet," Jason said.

They looked at each other, not even needing to say it.

If they were going to race in the all-important Sponsors' Event at the weekend, they had to win Race 25 on Thursday.

Second wouldn't cut it anymore.

Now they had to *win*.

The next few days went by very quickly.

Luckily, the weather brightened, and while Races 23 and 24 were still canceled, Race 25 was cleared to go ahead as scheduled on Thursday.

Scott Syracuse continued with lessons, even going so far as to schedule new classes on the days that had previously been set aside for Races 23 and 24. Most of the other teams had been given those days to rest or work on their cars at their leisure.

It was odd then that on the Tuesday—the original day for Race 24—*both* Horatio Wong and Isaiah Washington fell mysteriously ill, and so missed Syracuse's new classes.

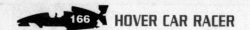

Tired as they were, Jason, the Bug, and Sally still went.

That same day, the format for Race 25 was revealed.

Put simply, Race 25—the halfway race in the school season—was a doozy.

It was an enduro, an eight-hour marathon on the school's second-longest course, a multifaceted track that snaked its way around the island of Tasmania, hugging the coastline, occasionally jutting inland. Since each lap would take an astonishing twenty-four minutes, the race was only twenty laps long. But this course came with two very special features.

The first feature was a worthy imitation of the signature feature of the Italian Run: *a shortcut*.

The famous shortcut in the Italian Run sliced through the heel of the "boot" that is Italy. As such, the term for successfully exploiting such a shortcut is: "cutting the heel."

The Race School's shortcut sliced across the main isthmus of the Port Arthur peninsula at the town of Dunalley, offering the game racer a 30-second jump on the rest of the pack—*if* he or she could figure out the correct route through a short underground maze.

And the second feature: ***demagnetizing ripple strips*** on all the hairpin turns and S-bend sections of the course.

Colloquially known as "demon lights," demagnetizing ripple strips are a standard feature on the pro tour and particularly nasty. They flank the curves on a hover car course and look rather like wide runway lights that float in the air.

Put simply, they are a method of enforcing disciplined driving. If you stray off the aerial track and fly *even for a moment* over some demag lights, your magneto drives lose magnetic power at an exponential rate. Thus your car loses traction and control. Dealing with demag lights is simple: don't run over them.

Since Wong and Washington weren't around, Jason, the Bug, and Sally took the opportunity to talk to Syracuse about tactics for Thursday's all-important race.

"What about the shortcut?" Jason asked. "Should we try to cut the heel?"

"No," Syracuse said quickly. "The shortcut is fool's gold. It looks like a good option, but in truth it's not an option at all."

"What if we're behind and it's the only chance we have?"

"I still wouldn't go near it," Syracuse said. "It's a trap for the unwise, for those who *like* shortcuts. Indeed, it's designed to appeal to their greed. I would only use it if I knew the correct way through it beforehand."

"But we *can't* know that," Sally said. "The peninsula mine tunnels are strictly out of bounds. We're not allowed to check them out beforehand."

Scott Syracuse cocked his head sideways. "No, Ms. McDuff. That's not entirely true. There *are* legitimate ways of mastering such mazes, if you have the patience . . ."

He left the sentence unfinished, looked directly at them.

"Unless you know the secret of the maze, I would suggest you not use the shortcut in Thursday's race."

With that they finished early, around 2:30 P.M.

Jason and the Bug returned to their dorm—weary, beat.

Truth be told, at that moment, Jason was feeling as low as he had ever felt at Race School. He felt overtired from too many classes, underappreciated by his teacher, out of his depth with his fellow racers, and out of races to win.

Which was probably why he was caught off-guard when he and the Bug arrived back at their apartment to find a pair of visitors waiting outside their dorm room, large shadows at the end of the hall.

At first Jason froze, fearing another confrontation with Xavier and Barnaby, but then he heard one of the shadows speak:

"*Where's* my little Doodlebug!" a booming woman's voice echoed down the corridor.

He smiled broadly.

There, standing outside his and the Bug's dorm room, were their parents.

The Chaser family went out for the afternoon.

They drove out to the ruins of the mighty eighteenth-century convict prison at the tip of the Port Arthur peninsula, where Martha Chaser unrolled a picnic blanket and spread out an array of sandwiches and soft drinks.

And Jason and the Bug spent a wonderful afternoon sitting in the sunshine talking with their parents.

The Bug sat nestled alongside Martha Chaser, looking very content, while Jason told their parents about everything that had happened to them at the International Race School since he and the Bug had last e-mailed.

He told them about their continuing technical problems, about recent races, about the Black Prince and Barnaby's backroom thuggery (which Martha didn't like at all and wanted to inform the authorities about, but to Jason's relief Henry Chaser stopped her by saying, "No, dear, this is a battle for the boys to fight"), and about Scott Syracuse's relentless class schedule that didn't seem to be replicated by any of the other teachers at the School.

He also told them about Race 25, the race that he and the Bug had to win if they were to get a start in Saturday's all-important tournament.

"First of all, son," Henry Chaser said gently, "let me just say this about your teacher, Mr. Syracuse. Never *ever* worry about having the "hard" teacher. Trust me, the hard teachers are always the best teachers."

"Why?"

"Because the hard teachers *want you to learn*. This Syracuse guy isn't here to be your best friend, Jason. He isn't here to have a fun old time. He's here to *teach*. And it sounds to me like he's teaching as hard as he can. What about you: Are you *learning* as hard as you can?"

Jason frowned at that. "But he never says 'well done' or 'good job.'"

"Ah-ha. So that's it," Henry Chaser said. "You want to get some positive feedback out of him. Want to know how to get that?"

"Yes."

Henry Chaser smiled enigmatically. "Jason. When you start learning as hard as you can, I guarantee he'll start treating you differently."

Jason sighed, bowed his head.

His father clapped him on the shoulder. "It's okay, son. You're only fourteen. You've got to learn these things sometime. Now. To more important matters. Tell me again about this race on Thursday that you have to win at all costs."

★ ★ ★

Unfortunately the afternoon had to end, and as dusk descended, the Chasers packed up their stuff and started the drive back to the Race School.

On the way back, with the Bug fast asleep beside him, Jason gazed idly out the window of their car, watching the landscape whistle by.

As such, he wasn't really paying attention when Henry pulled over abruptly—to help a biker on the side of the road.

Jason watched as his father, illuminated by the headlights of their car, walked over to the young man crouched beside his bike.

Jason couldn't see the biker's face, but he noticed that the man's hover motorcycle—a nice Kawasaki XT-700 trail rider—was completely covered in a strange gray powder.

"Need a hand, partner?" Henry Chaser said into the darkness. "Or a ride?"

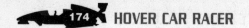

The biker waved him off. His riding leathers were also, Jason noticed, totally covered in the gray powder.

"Nah. Just fixed it," the biker called. "Got some dust in the mag switches."

Sure enough, he had fixed the problem. The young man's bike hummed to life and he straddled the hover cycle, reaching for his helmet.

And in that instant, Jason saw the young man's face.

Then the hover bike raced off into the night, and Henry Chaser returned to the car, shrugging.

Jason, however, sat frozen in his seat.

He had recognized the biker.

It was Wernold Smythe, the clerk from the Race School's Department.

"Sounds like it'll be a tough race," Henry Chaser said as he dropped Jason and Bug off at the Race School. Henry and Martha were going to stay at a trailer park in Hobart for a few days and watch Thursday's big race.

Henry said, "Eight hours means a lot of pit stops—your mech chief is in for a long day. And stay away from those demon lights. Run over some of those and your race is over. And watch out for other drivers ramming you onto them. Oh, and Jason . . ."

"Yes, Dad?"

"Always remember the Bradbury Principle."

"Yes, Dad," Jason sighed. His father *always* said that. It was Henry Chaser's contribution to sport: the Bradbury Principle. Jason ignored it and got serious: "What do you think about cutting the heel?"

"Wouldn't touch it," Henry said. "The pros rarely cut the heel in the Italian Run and for good reason. It's a Venus flytrap: looks pretty and alluring from the outside, but it'll just eat you up. It'll put you either further behind or out of the running completely."

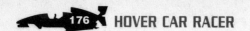

"That's just what Mr. Syracuse said," Jason said.

"Scott Syracuse said the same thing?" Henry said. "Oh! Of course—" He cut himself off, chuckled.

"What?" Jason asked.

Henry Chaser smiled. "Scott Syracuse once tried to cut the heel in the Italian Run. It was the last time he raced the Italian Run; a few races later, he had that huge crash in New York that ended his career.

"That time in Italy, Syracuse was way back in the pack because of a collision he'd had with another car, so he decided to try and cut the heel. Now, if you cut the heel in Italy, you can gain up to *four whole minutes* on the rest of the field. It woulda put him back in contention."

"And what happened?" Jason asked.

"Two *hours* later, the race was over and he still hadn't come out," Henry said. "He didn't emerge until *four hours* after the race, and even then, he came out the way he went in. Didn't even find the way through. By the time he reached the Finish Line in Venice, they were dismantling the grandstands! No wonder he advises against cutting the heel."

"Yeah," Jason said, frowning. "No wonder."

THE INTERNATIONAL
RACE SCHOOL
RACE 25: SUPER-ENDURO
(with short cut)

▬▬▬▬	Course 7
▐▐▐▐▐▐	Demagnetising Strip
▐▐▐▐▐▐	Short cut

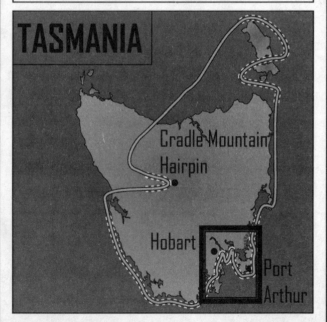

TASMANIA

Cradle Mountain
Hairpin

Hobart

Port
Arthur

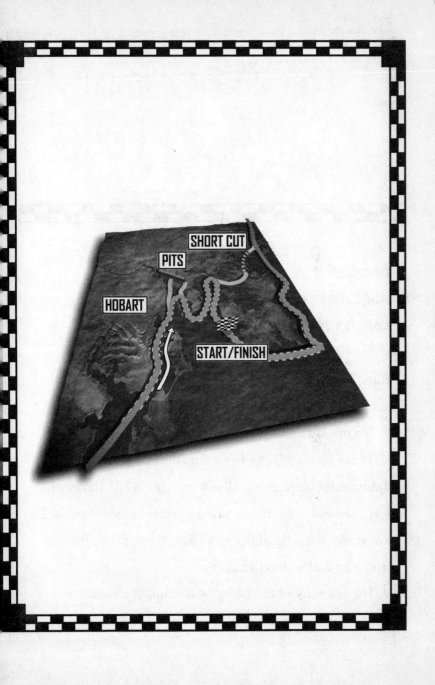

RACE 25

RACETIME: 4 HOURS 24 MINS

LAP: 11 [OF 20]

Race 25 was easily the most hard-fought race of the season so far.

No one was giving an inch.

Those racers who hadn't yet qualified for the Sponsors' Tournament were going all-out to win. While those who *had* qualified were racing just as fiercely—they were well aware that if a prequalified racer won, it meant one less contender to deal with on Saturday.

The intensity of the racing was simply furious.

And at Lap 11, Jason was still in it.

After narrowly avoiding a wild three-car crash on Lap 2, he had kept pace with the early leaders—Xavier, Varishna Krishna (a talented young racer from India), and Isaiah Washington—and now, after more than four hours of racing, he was well positioned in 4th place.

The ripple strips had caused chaos—if you took a turn too wide, you would edge over the top of them and suddenly your magneto drive levels would drain before your eyes.

The big crash on Lap 2 had been the direct result of the ripple strips, and it had taken out some of the contenders in this race.

It was Barnaby Becker's fault.

He had slid out over the ripple strips flanking the tight hairpin near the pits. He had stayed over the demag strips for almost five seconds, enough to deprive *all six* of his magneto drives of nearly all their power. Out of control, he had slid back across the track, collecting two other racers—among them Ariel Piper—on the way through, ending all of their races.

Ariel wasn't pleased.

For his part, Jason felt he was handling the strips pretty well—not perfectly, but well. On any given lap, he might edge over a couple of them and lose a little bit of power. But judging by the similarity of their pit-stop schedules, it didn't seem as if any of the other contenders were doing any better.

Significantly, no racer had attempted to use the shortcut.

The leaders completed Lap 11, and flocked into the pits— Jason among them.

He swung into his bay and the Tarantula descended on the *Argonaut* from above, its arms bristling with magneto drives and coolant hoses.

Jason gulped down some energy drink, breathed hard.

Their pit stops had been good in this race. Their mag drives and computer systems seemed okay—

And suddenly the Tarantula froze in midaction.

"No!" Jason yelled.

Sally McDuff dived for the Tarantula's console, started tapping keys. "The system's crashed again!" she yelled. "Bugger! I have to reboot!"

She typed fast on the computer.

Jason snapped round—

—to see Krishna, then Washington, and then Xavier zoom out of the pits, one after the other, rejoining the race.

"Sally! Come on!"

"Almost there . . . !" she called back. "Almost there!"

"Dang it!"

The seconds ticked by—every one of them sinking the nails deeper into Jason's coffin.

10 seconds . . .

15 . . .

20 . . .

"Got it!" Sally called.

The Tarantula completed its work, then swooped up into the ceiling and Sally yelled "Go! Go! Go!" and Jason floored it and the *Argonaut* shoomed back out onto the course—

—to be met by a surprising sight.

Just outside Pit Lane, Jason saw Car No. 1—Prince Xavier's black Lockheed, the *Speed Razor*—splayed sideways in the center of the track, stopped. Xavier was waving his fists at an orange hover car that had crashed into the treeline nearby.

Jason deduced what had happened immediately.

As Xavier had been exiting the pits, the hapless driver of the orange car—a perennial straggler named Brent

Hurst—had been zooming by, completely unaware of Xavier emerging from Pit Lane. A near-miss had ensued, with the *Speed Razor* fishtailing to a halt, while Hurst had missed the next turn, hit the ripple strips, and gone careering off into the treeline.

By the time Jason had emerged from the pits shortly after, Xavier was powering up, so the two of them rejoined the race together, 20 seconds behind the leaders, with the *Speed Razor* just in front of the *Argonaut*.

Over the next three laps, try as he might, Jason couldn't narrow the gap on the leaders.

There was another pit stop, but since everyone was pitting more or less as well as each other, the lead time between the two leaders—Krishna and Washington—and the rest of the pack, led by Xavier and Jason, remained at about 20 seconds.

It was with the completion of Lap 14 that Jason realized.

He was running out of laps.

There were only six laps to go, with most racers planning for two more stops, and he wasn't gaining at all.

This was terrible. With an enormous 20-second gap to reel in, he just couldn't win—and he *had* to win this race!

Unless . . .

"Sally! Bug!" he yelled into his radiomike. "Quick poll! Next lap, do we try the shortcut?"

"Jason, I don't know . . ." Sally said. *"If you screw it up in there, we'll lose for sure."*

"We're already going to lose!" Jason said. "Unless we get some galactic good luck. Bug?"

The Bug whispered his reply.

"That bad, huh?" Jason said. "Are there any stats you *don't* know, little brother?"

The Bug's analysis didn't give him confidence. Only one hover car racer had ever actually won a pro race by successfully utilizing a shortcut maze—out of 165

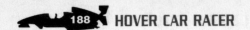

shortcut-equipped races. Not good odds.

"We're screwed," Jason said aloud.

The laps ticked over: 15, 16 . . .

The lead gap remained 20 seconds.

Crap, Jason thought, he couldn't even get past the Black Prince.

Lap 16 saw more pit stops.

Krishna and Washington were leaving the pits just as Xavier and Jason swept into them.

As the Tarantula went to work, Jason looked over at Xavier's busy pit bay.

In the midst of all the activity around the *Speed Razor,* Jason saw Xavier chatting animatedly with his mech chief, Oliver Koch. And beyond it all, Jason saw someone else standing at the back of their bay, a young man who wasn't wearing the charcoal-black uniform of the *Speed Razor*'s team—

Jason froze.

The young man standing in the very back of Xavier's pit bay was Wernold Smythe.

"Hey, Sally," Jason said. "How long has Werny Smythe been in Xavier's pit bay?"

"He arrived a few laps ago. Started talking to Koch about something."

Jason looked back at *Speed Razor*'s pit bay: saw Xavier and Koch talking. Koch was making sharp hand gestures, as if he were giving Xavier detailed directions.

Then Jason checked out Wernold Smythe again. He remembered seeing Smythe two nights ago, by the side of the road, covered in gray powder, with his hover bike similarly covered.

And suddenly it hit Jason.

"Bug! The shortcut at Dunalley. It's an abandoned mine, right?"

The Bug said that it was.

"What kind of mine?"

The Bug said that it had been a coal mine.

"A coal mine . . ." Jason said. "Limestone powder . . ."

"Jason? What are you thinking?" Sally asked.

Jason said, "Coal mines use limestone powder to guard against flammable gases oozing out from the walls. It's a gray powder that miners spray all over the walls of a mine. Covers everything. I read about it in a thriller novel once."

"So?"

"So, I happened to see Werny on Tuesday night, out on the road to Port Arthur, completely covered in gray powder . . ."

And with those words the picture became clear in Jason's mind.

"That's what Koch and Xavier were paying Werny for!" he exclaimed. "They weren't paying Werny to give us faulty parts. Koch and Xavier were paying Werny to go out and map the shortcut for them, to find a way through it! Holy cow, guys, we just got galactically lucky."

Voom!

The *Speed Razor* blasted out of the pits—just as the Tarantula lifted up and away from the *Argonaut.*

His face set, Jason jammed his thrusters forward and took off after Xavier as though his life depended on it.

Prince Xavier's *Speed Razor* blasted out of the pits pursued by the *Argonaut.*

The pits were situated right on the mouth of the Derwent River, in the middle of the course's most fiendish section of hairpin turns, each of which was skirted by demagnetizing ripple strips.

Xavier ripped around the first turn, a sharp left-hander, banking steeply, closely followed by Jason in the *Argonaut.*

The next turn was a tight right-hander—and the point at which racers could take the option of cutting the heel of the Port Arthur peninsula at the Dunalley isthmus.

Right on cue, Prince Xavier took the alternative route and charged *left*, leaving the course proper, going for the shortcut.

The crowds in the mobile hover stands gasped.

That the leaders had already taken the longer and safer route made the move daring in itself. But that it was Prince Xavier Xonora—dashing and handsome and the championship leader—who had decided to go for it thrilled them even more.

But then something even more astonishing happened.

The *Argonaut* took off after the *Speed Razor*, zooming toward the shortcut behind it.

The two cars rushed toward the Dunalley isthmus. As he flew, Jason could see the wide blue ocean beyond the narrow strip of land.

But in the foreground, built into the front edge of the isthmus like a cannon emplacement—as if guarding the way—yawned the squat concrete entry tunnel to the shortcut mine.

The *Speed Razor* didn't hesitate. It disappeared into the mine at 190 mph.

Jason swallowed. He had to stay close to Xavier—since Xavier knew the way through.

The black entry tunnel to the mine rushed toward him like the open mouth of a hungry giant. Jason drew in a sharp breath.

"Hang on, Bug. Here we go!"

And with that the *Argonaut* shot underground, disappearing into the blackness of the mine.

THE SHORTCUT LABYRINTH
LAP: 17 [OF 20]

Rocketing through darkness.

The close square walls of the abandoned mine whipped past Jason at astonishing speed, the whole underground world illuminated only by the sabrelike beams of his headlights. Each tunnel was about the width and height of an old railway tunnel.

Up ahead, he saw the glowing red taillights of the *Speed Razor* descending into the bowels of the Earth, following the steep entry tunnel straight down. Then

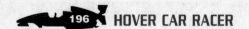

without warning, the red lights cut left, having arrived at the bottom of the entry tunnel.

Jason shot off after them. He had to keep those taillights in view—

The Bug said something.

"I know! I know!" Jason yelled back. "I'm trying to stay with him!"

The *Speed Razor* banked momentarily out of sight, and Jason followed it, only to find himself staring at a fork of two tunnels . . . and no taillights in sight.

A bolt of ice shot up Jason's spine.

No . . .

Then he saw the taillights way up the right-hand fork and relief swept through him and he took off after them.

The mine flattened out and the *Speed Razor* raced through it at rocket speed, taking turns easily, a sharp left here, a sweeping right there, with the *Argonaut* close behind it.

And then Jason noticed that the tunnels had started to slant upward. They were approaching the surface. Trailing close behind the *Speed Razor*, he rounded a final bend before—

—blinding sunlight assaulted his eyes.

They were out!

They'd got through the shortcut maze.

The eastern coastline of Tasmania stretched gloriously away to the left, with Prince Xavier's *Speed Razor* rocketing away along it.

The *Argonaut* blasted out of a trapezoidal pipe halfway up the coastal cliffs and banked sharply to avoid the specially placed set of demagnetizing strips at the junction of the shortcut and the regular course, just as—

shoom! shoom!—two cars boomed past him on either side.

Varishna Krishna and Isaiah Washington!

The former race leaders!

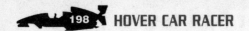

And suddenly Jason's eyes widened.

Thanks to the Black Prince, the *Argonaut* was back in the race.

The next lap and a half saw some of the fiercest racing of Jason's life.

Through the S-bends up at the top-right corner of Tasmania, winding between Cape Barren Island and Flinders Island—trying to avoid the demag strips while also trying to overtake his foes.

And then Varishna Krishna tried to slip past Xavier at the hairpin next to Pit Lane, but Xavier cruelly blocked him, forcing the Indian out over the ripple strips.

Krishna reeled, skidding wide, and as he did so, Washington managed to slip past him into 2nd place. Jason tried to snatch the opportunity as well, but Krishna regained control of his car at exactly the wrong time, and not only did he shut Jason out, he also made him slow down a fraction.

Jason swore.

And so, by Lap 18, with only two laps to go, he was still in 4th place, in what was now essentially a four-horse race, behind three of the best drivers in the school: Xavier, Washington, and Krishna.

With the race almost eight hours old now, everyone was running on depleted mags, depleted nerves, and depleted energy levels. The sheer intensity of their battle had meant that all of the top four racers had at some point touched the ripple strips in the last few laps, thus further losing traction.

Which meant, with two laps to go and their magneto drives starting to feel slippery, they'd each need to make one last pit stop.

★ ★ ★

Halfway round Lap 18, Sally McDuff's voice came through Jason's earpiece.

"Jason! The other crews are preparing for their final pit stop. You wanna come in with them now or wait till the next lap?"

Jason pursed his lips, assessed the situation.

His magneto drive levels were at 39 percent of full strength. Two laps on this course would consume about 30 percent: 15 percent per lap. The remaining 9 percent allowed him maybe three bumps on the ripple strips.

You have to win. Second place isn't an option today.

The Bug seemed to read his mind, and said so.

"Thirty-nine percent. We can make it . . ." Jason said.

The Bug was doubtful.

Sally, listening in on the radio, said: *"Jason, no. Not again. Don't even think it."*

"They won't be expecting it," Jason said.

"Jason, it didn't work in that training race with Wong and

Washington. And you remember Syracuse's stats. Skipping the last pit stop has a success rate of 0.005 percent."

At that moment, the Bug reminded Jason of another piece of Scott Syracuse's wisdom: *To err is human, to make the same mistake twice is stupid.*

Jason's eyes narrowed.

"We're gonna do it."

And so, as the three lead cars decelerated into the pits for their final pit stops, to the absolute amazement of the crowds, the *Argonaut* swept past the pit entry and zoomed off down the track, trying to put as much distance between it and its rivals before they came out of the pits, hungry to chase him down.

Jason hit the shortcut tunnel on the fly and, guided by the Bug's photographic memory of their previous trip through the labyrinth, took the same route they'd taken before.

They emerged from the other side, banking a little too wildly, and Jason touched the demag strips on the outside of the track and his magneto drive levels dropped 3 percent.

"*The others are out of the pits now, Jason!*" Sally's voice warned in his ear. "*They're hunting you down!*"

The *Argonaut* swept round the course.

Jason concentrated intensely.

His magneto counter ticked steadily downward.

The other three cars gained on him, rocketing round the course on fresh mags. But Washington and Krishna didn't have the nerve to follow Xavier through the short-cut tunnel and they fell behind, taking the long way around, and in doing so, effectively put themselves out of the running.

The Black Prince, however, took the tunnel fearlessly, and as such, he kept gaining on the *Argonaut*.

Then, on the other side of the course, Jason hit the demag strips bounding the Cradle Mountain hairpin, just a glancing blow, but enough to send his mag meter whizzing down another 3 percent.

The *Speed Razor* kept coming. On the long straight-aways, Jason could see it looming in the distance in his mirrors.

Mag levels: 18 percent.

The *Argonaut* came to the sharp hairpins near the pits. Despite the fact that he took them extra carefully, to Jason's horror, he clipped the ripple strip on the super-sharp right-hand hairpin just before the Start-Finish Line and suddenly his mag levels were at a bare 15 percent.

Jason knew what that meant.

With only one lap to go, on ever-declining mags, and with a ruthless competitor looming up behind him on a fresh set of magneto drives, he had to do a perfect lap.

LAP: 20 [OF 20]

The *Argonaut* cut left, banking toward the shortcut isthmus, commencing the final lap.

The crowds in the stands were on the edge of their seats. Among them, Henry Chaser sat with his hand held to his mouth. Martha Chaser seemed quite content beside him, head bowed, doing some knitting.

The *Argonaut* raced into the shortcut tunnel for the last time. The *Speed Razor* also banked left, heading for the isthmus, starting the final lap. The *Argonaut* zoomed up the coast. The *Speed Razor* entered the shortcut mine. The *Argonaut* zigzagged between the upper islands. The *Speed Razor* roared up the coast.

At Cradle Mountain, Jason slowed dramatically to take the turn that had cost him some magnetism on the previous lap. The *Argonaut* was sliding all over the place now, handling like someone trying to walk on an ice skating rink, going at a torturously slow 280 mph.

The *Speed Razor* was doing 375 mph and accelerating.

Halfway round and Jason's mag levels were down to 7.5 percent. Just enough to get home—if he didn't touch any ripple strips.

Down the wild western coast of Tasmania—with the *Speed Razor* now looming large in his mirrors.

Xavier's car moved surely and securely, always gaining. The *Argonaut* slipped and slid, limping home.

Everyone could see where this was heading.

At their current speeds, the *Speed Razor* was going to catch the *Argonaut* right at the death.

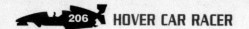

Mag levels: 3 percent

Jason floored it down the last long sweeper, bracing himself for the series of dreadfully tight hairpins guarding the Finish Line—hairpins that he was going to have to negotiate perfectly. One touch on the ripple strips now would end his race.

Mag levels: 2 percent

"Come on . . ." he willed himself. "Come *on* . . ."

Prince Xavier's black Lockheed now filled his mirrors.

The *Argonaut* took the left-hander into Storm Bay at a pathetic 210 mph. Glowing red demag lights whizzed by it on either side. The *Speed Razor* took the same turn a split-second later, doing 280. The *Argonaut* shot past the pits, slowed to a crawl to take the first right-hand hairpin. The *Speed Razor* launched itself into the same turn.

The two cars were almost level.

Mag levels: 1 percent.

Jason swung left, into the second-to-last turn of the race—a left-hand hairpin—just as the *Speed Razor* came alongside his tail.

Then it was into the last corner of the race, a tight right-hand hairpin, and here Xavier made his move, tried to overtake Jason *on the outside!*

The two cars roared round the final turn *side by side.*

Henry Chaser leaped to his feet. Sally McDuff prayed before her monitor.

The crowds in the stands rose as one.

And the two hover cars—the blue, white, and silver Car 55 and the all-black Car 1—whipped out of the last turn, rocketed down the home straightaway, and, in a blur of speed, crossed the line together.

LAP: 20 [OF 20]

To the naked eye, it appeared as if the two cars had crossed the Finish Line together, but the official laser digital photo of the finish of Race 25 would later show that after eight hours of racing, after twenty hard-fought laps, Car No. 1, the *Speed Razor*, driven by Xonora X, traveling at 230 miles an hour and accelerating, had crossed the line 1.64 inches behind Car No. 55, the *Argonaut*, piloted by Chaser J., and traveling at 200 miles an hour.

After a perfect lap from its daring young driver, by the paintwork on its nosewing, the *Argonaut* had qualified for the Sponsors' Tournament.

ACKNOWLEDGMENTS

Hi there, Readers!

As you will quickly notice, there are a couple of entirely new things about Hover Car Racer: the race maps and the illustrations. While I've always had maps and diagrams in my books, with Hover Car Racer I knew I'd need something more than I'd ever seen in a novel before. Fortunately for me, this gave me the opportunity to work with one of Australia's finest graphic designers, a young man from Brisbane named Roy Govier, from Xiphos.

While Roy had previously designed the missile on the cover of Scarecrow, this was a much bigger task. For six months, he took my (let's face it, pretty pathetic) sketches and turned them into awesome 3-dimensional race maps. I thank him for his huge efforts.

As for the illustrations, well, what can I say. They really do speak for themselves. I think Pablo Raimondi has brought the ideas that once resided only in my head completely to life. From the very first picture of the *Argonaut* being hit by mini-meteorites, Pablo just "got" Hover Car Racer: got the sheer velocity of it.

Beyond that, as always, there are many others to thank: the wonderful team at Pan Macmillan (in Australia) and Simon & Schuster (in the United States). In Australia they are led by my incredible publisher, Cate Paterson (who has pretty well become the godmother of mass-market fiction in this country). Jane Novak: my fantastic publicist. Sarina Rowell: my hardworking editor. Behind the scenes, I am also indebted to Ross Gibb, Paul Kenny, Jeannine Fowler, and James Fraser for their guidance and experience. And at Simon & Schuster, I am indebted to Kevin Lewis, the man who put the *bling* into hover car racing. His vision for the U.S. edition of this book has been extraordinary. And, of course, my sincere thanks once again to all the sales reps at Pan Macmillan who visit bookstores every day to sell my books.

Publishing is a team game, and they are a sensational team.

And, lastly, the greatest thanks of all must go to my wife, Natalie. I remember when she came home from work one day and found me, an allegedly grown man, surrounded by an absolute mess—model parts, glue, paint all over my hands-and I held up the very first model of the Argonaut and said: "Look what I made! A hover car!" Or the other time when she came home from work and found half of the living room submerged beneath a giant seven-foot-tall styrofoam model of a Mayan pyramid. In both cases, she just smiled at me and said, "That's great!" Every writer should have this kind of encouragement. No, seriously, this is why I have said before: to anyone who knows a writer, never underestimate the power of your encourage-ment. Thanks, Nat!

Now, enough with all that. It's time to race!

MR
Sydney, Australia

ABOUT THE AUTHOR AND ILLUSTRATOR

Matthew Reilly is the author of five hit adult novels, including *Contest,* the *New York Times* bestseller *Area 7, Temple,* the worldwide bestseller *Ice Station,* and most recently, *Scarecrow.* Australian born, he wrote his first two novels while studying law at the University of New South Wales. He now writes full-time, creating screenplays and television series in addition to novels. Matthew lives in Sydney, Australia, and can be visited on the Internet at www.matthewreilly.com.

A native of Argentina, **Pablo Raimondi** moved to the United States to pursue his dream of creating comic books. These days Pablo earns his keep by capturing the high-flying, death-defying deeds of superheroes for Marvel and DC Comics, and he has lent his considerable talent to the exploits of Superman, Batman, and the X-Men. His work was most recently seen in Marvel's incredibly well reviewed X-Men/X-Factor spin-off miniseries, *Madrox.* Pablo lives in New York City.